OTHER BOOKS by KASSANDRA LAMB

The Kate Huntington Mystery Series:
MULTIPLE MOTIVES
ILL-TIMED ENTANGLEMENTS
FAMILY FALLACIES
CELEBRITY STATUS
COLLATERAL CASUALTIES
ZERO HERO
FATAL FORTY-EIGHT
SUICIDAL SUSPICIONS

The Kate On Vacation Mystery Series (novellas):
An Unsaintly Season in St. Augustine
Cruel Capers on the Caribbean
Ten-Gallon Tensions in Texas
Missing on Maui
(coming Summer, 2016)

The Marcia Banks and Buddy Mystery Series:
To Kill A Labrador
Arsenic and Young Lacy
(coming Fall, 2016)

ECHOES, A Story of Suspense
(a stand-alone ghost story/mystery)

TO KILL A LABRADOR

A Marcia Banks and Buddy Mystery

Kassandra Lamb

To Kill A Labrador
A Marcia Banks and Buddy Mystery

Published in the United States of America by misterio press,
a Florida limited liability company
http://misteriopress.com

First Edition

To Kill A Labrador is a work of fiction. All names, characters, and events are products of the author's imagination (as are most of the places). Any resemblance to actual events or people, living or dead, is entirely coincidental. Some real places have been used fictitiously. The towns of Mayfair, Florida and Collinsville, Florida are fictitious.

~~~~~~~~~~~

Edited by Marcy Kennedy

Cover and interior design by Melinda VanLone, Book Cover Corner

Photo credits: Labrador pup with flag by Tracy Hornbrook; silhouette of woman and dog by Majivecka
(right of use purchased from dreamstime.com)

ISBN 13: 978-0-9908747-8-2 (misterio press LLC)
ISBN 10: 0-9908747-8-8
~~~~~~~~~~~

Again, to my friend Angi,
without whom none of my books
would have ever seen the light of day.

~~~

And to Shannon,
my good friend and partner in misterio press.
~~~

CHAPTER ONE

I'm a normal person. Granted I have a somewhat abnormal vocation. I train service animals for PTSD sufferers–mostly combat veterans.

But other than that, I'm just a small-town, thirty-something divorcee.

My name is Marcia Banks–pronounced Mar-see-a, not Marsha. Okay, okay, so I don't have a totally normal name.

I live in central Florida, on the outskirts of the Ocala National Forest, in a little town called Mayfair, population 258 (and a half. Agnes Baker's pregnant. Again.)

Mayfair sprang up in the 1960s, due to the transitory success of the Mayfair Alligator Farm (rumor has it that old Mr. Mayfair poached the gators from the Forest). Billboards plastered along the newly minted I-75 corridor drew in unsuspecting vacationers to witness the wonders of gator wrestling and to purchase fake alligator skin handbags and belts. But the farm went under when Walt Disney plopped his amusement park down next to another sleepy Florida hamlet–Orlando.

Mayfair was virtually a ghost town when I moved here two years ago, shortly after the demise of my brief but disastrous marriage to a concert violinist in the Baltimore Symphony.

It's a great place to train service animals because everybody knows everybody. It didn't take long for the residents to learn the rules. The main one being to never, ever pet the dogs I'm training unless I say it's okay.

The exception is my Black Lab-Rottie mix, Buddy, *if* he's the only dog I'm walking at the time.

He was my first trainee, and how he came back into my possession was the beginning of my not-so-normal avocation–unwilling amateur sleuth.

One sunny day last winter, I received the most shocking phone call of my life. It even beat out the anonymous one three years ago informing me that my husband was having an affair with a cello player.

The caller said she was with the Collinsville Sheriff's Department and wanted to know if I had trained a service dog named Buddy.

My mind scrambled for a reason why someone from a sheriff's department would be asking me that. Had Buddy bit someone?

"Where exactly is Collinsville?" I asked, stalling for time.

"Off 33, near Polk City."

"In Florida?" More stalling.

"Yes, ma'am, not far from Lakeland." Her tone said she was losing patience with me. "Are you the Marcia Banks who trained Buddy?" She mispronounced my first name, of course.

I couldn't figure out how to get around admitting it, since I had signed off on his training certificate. "Uh, yes."

"Could ya come get the dog as soon as possible?"

"Why? What's happened to his owner?" Jimmy Garrett was an Iraqi veteran who'd had a close encounter with an IED. As a result, he'd come home with a prosthesis where his right leg used to be and some pretty disabling nightmares, among other PTSD symptoms.

"He's been arrested, ma'am."

"What about his wife?"

A long pause. "That's why he's been arrested. He's bein' held on suspicion of murder."

"Of his wife?" My voice rose, ending on a squeak.

"Yes, ma'am."

I was stunned. I'd spent a fair amount of time with the Garretts two years ago, teaching Jimmy the do's and don't's of working with a service dog. Mathilda Jones, the woman who had trained me to be a trainer, had drummed into me the importance of working with the client as well as the dog. *A poorly-trained human can ruin a well-trained dog* was her mantra. Humans was how Mattie referred to people, like we were a different species from herself. She seemed to feel more connected to her dogs than to two-legged *homo sapiens*.

I'd gotten the distinct impression that the Garretts had a stable and loving relationship. Julie, Jimmy's wife, had confided to me privately that she was so relieved he was getting Buddy. "We just want to get on with life," she'd said in a soft Southern accent. "His nightmares and everythin', they just make him so miserable. Just maybe things can settle down now and we can start a family." She'd then blushed and ducked her head.

Other than a mildly annoying predilection for the word *just*, she had seemed like a bright and kind person who was devoted to Jimmy, and he to her. I'd received a birth announcement eight months later. Apparently Ida Mae Garrett had already been a bun in the oven when Julie and I had that conversation.

"Are ya there, ma'am?" The woman from the sheriff's department yanked me back to the present.

"Yeah. Uh, I can probably get down there sometime this afternoon."

"Come to the sheriff's department. It's on Main Street."

I shook my head, trying to wrap my brain around the whole mess. "Okay. I've got to make some arrangements here. I'll be there as soon as I can."

Normally when I'm away from the house, the dogs are in their crates, but I didn't know how long I would be gone. It was close to a two-hour drive in each direction, and there might be some red tape involved. The friend who was my back-up person with the dogs had a full work schedule that afternoon, and a date that night. I hated to disrupt Becky's plans on the off chance that I might be gone longer than the dogs' bladders could handle.

I called my neighbor's house and was relieved when her college-student daughter, Sybil, answered. I asked her to come over if I wasn't back by nine and let the dogs out into my fenced backyard for a bathroom break.

I'd been prepared with a small fib if Sybil's mother, the reigning matriarch of the only African-American family in town, had answered. Sherie Wells could sniff out gossip like a bloodhound. But Sybil asked no questions. I told her I'd leave a key under the front doormat.

And no, I'm not a paranoid Northerner who's afraid to leave her door unlocked in a small town. I don't dare risk that a friendly neighbor might come calling and accidentally let the dogs get out.

It was a warm day for early February–already at seventy-five and climbing–so I threw on a clean, red tank top over my jeans and grabbed my favorite gray cardigan, the one with a little bit of flare at the bottom that disguises my all too ample hips. I opted to forego make-up, except for a swipe of lip gloss and some sun screen on my face. Even in the winter, the Florida sun could fry my fair skin in no time.

At the last minute, I crammed a pair of clean underwear and a stick of deodorant into my purse. I couldn't imagine I'd end up staying overnight in Collinsville, but then I never would have imagined before today that sweet Julie Garrett would be dead and poor Jimmy arrested for her murder. So all bets were off on what to expect from the universe right now.

By the time I got to Collinsville, I was glad I'd worn a tank top. The temperature, according to the sign on the Collinsville Bank, was now eighty.

The sheriff's department wasn't hard to find. It was the most rundown building on Main Street, with gray peeling paint and a rusty metal roof.

The inside didn't look much better. The walls were the same gray as the exterior, although they weren't peeling. A small waiting area contained metal folding chairs, the only wall adornment a large bulletin board plastered with mug shots of nasty-looking men and women and heartbreakingly sweet pictures of missing children. A hand-printed heading read *Have You Seen These People?* I suspected the wanted posters were from the whole central Florida area. Surely there weren't that many felons on the loose in this podunk town.

An air compressor rumbled somewhere, but the building's air conditioning was apparently as old as the paint job on the outside. The room was muggy with humidity. If the AC wasn't keeping up today, what kind of oven did this place become in the summer?

Behind a chest-high Formica counter was a woman in a khaki sheriff's department uniform. She either had very long legs or she was sitting on a stool. Her dark eyebrows said the blonde of her hair was out of a bottle. She was too thin, with the leathery skin of a long-term Florida resident.

"Can I help ya?" Her accent confirmed her as a Florida native, her voice beginning to take on the raspiness of a long-time smoker. She scratched absently at a forearm covered by a long khaki sleeve. Perspiration beaded on her upper lip.

I wondered why she hadn't rolled her sleeves up, then mentally shrugged. Maybe it was against departmental rules.

"I'm Marcia Banks, Buddy's trainer."

"Oh yeah. Ya know where the Garretts' house is? The mutt's still there, last I heard." There was a slight sneer in her voice. Not a dog person, apparently.

"Uh, I'm not sure." The house I had delivered Buddy to two years ago wasn't all that far from here, but it wasn't in the town of Collinsville.

"I'll write down the address." She ducked her head over a pad of paper.

"Is Jimmy here? Could I see him?" I heard the words exit my mouth and wondered where the heck they had come from. Did I really want to see Jimmy Garrett? There was nothing I could do to help him.

The full ramifications of Jimmy's situation hit me in the gut. He'd been doing so well. What happened?

The woman behind the counter was staring at me, an inscrutable expression on her face. "I guess it'd be okay." She slid off her stool and almost disappeared behind the counter.

Her disembodied head nodded toward the left. "Go to that door over there."

I followed instructions. A click and then she pulled the door open.

"Ya have to leave your purse here with me."

I turned it over to her, and she placed it on a shelf under the counter.

"Follow me." She led me down a long gray corridor that ended in the jail section of the building–two cells on the right and one larger one around a small corner on the left.

Jimmy was the only occupant. He was in the larger cell. It contained a cot and small table, both bolted to the floor, and a metal toilet.

When he caught sight of me, he raced over and grabbed the bars. "Marcia, thank God you came. You gotta take Buddy for a while."

"I can do that." I scraped back a long strand of hair that had escaped from my ponytail.

Jimmy wore a faded Marines T-shirt and dark running shorts. I averted my eyes from his prosthesis. Despite all the time I'd spent with combat vets, I still wasn't used to seeing a metal contraption sticking out where bone and flesh should be.

"Doris, could I speak to Ms. Banks alone, please." Technically it was a request, but his commanding tone hinted at the sergeant he had once been.

The woman, Doris, gave him a dirty look, then turned on her sensible oxford's heel and stalked away.

"Marcia, I need your help. The whole town's gonna be just like her. They're gonna turn against me and I won't have a chance."

Unsure how to answer him, I stalled. "What happened?" Okay,

I was also dying of curiosity.

Jimmy ran a hand over his buzz cut of light brown hair. "I wish I knew. Nobody'll tell me nothin' except that Julie…" His voice choked a little on his wife's name. "That she's dead and I'm being held for her murder." His face contorted, but then he shook himself, like a dog waking up from a bad dream.

"Buddy and I went for our morning run. We stopped for a bit to watch the ducks down by the pond in the park. When I got back, I came in the front door and saw Ida Mae playin' in her pack-and-play in the corner. And that's the last thing I remember until I woke up on the floor. Buddy was standin' over me growlin' and Ida Mae was cryin'. And the deputies were in the doorway yellin' at me to control the dog."

He scrubbed his stubbled face with a broad hand. "They said Julie was in the bedroom…" His voice caught again. "But they wouldn't let me see her. They say I was drunk and we musta argued, but honest, I haven't had a drink in months. Me and the beer, we were gettin' too friendly, so I stopped completely."

He ducked his head. "I've been goin' to AA the next town over."

I sucked in air, trying to think of something to say, and picked up a whiff of stale beer. But Jimmy didn't act like someone who was lying. Of course, I was no expert on lying, nor on Jimmy Garrett. For all I knew he was a pathological liar.

"I can take Buddy for a while, until this mess gets resolved. But I don't know what else I can do. I'm a dog trainer."

Jimmy shook his head and kept talking, as if I hadn't said anything. "This is Julie's hometown. We moved here awhile after the baby was born, 'cause Julie had a good job at the bank. Everybody's treated me fine, but I'm still the outsider. They're gonna turn on me, I just know it."

I'd always thought Jimmy was a local boy too, since he had a Southern accent. "Aren't you from Florida?"

"Tennessee. I was in advanced training at the Naval Air Base in Pensacola when Julie and I met. She was goin' to UWF."

It took me a moment to decipher UWF. There's a whole slew of universities around Florida that are U something F. Since the other abbreviations–UNF, UCF, USF–all referred to geographical locations, I deduced that UWF was University of West Florida.

"Okay, so you're not local and this is a small town," I said, "but I don't think they're going to railroad you into a murder conviction if you didn't do it."

The small towns I'd encountered in Florida were not nearly as insular as small towns elsewhere tended to be. There were so many transplants from other parts of the country, especially the cold north, that only about a half to three-quarters of the residents, even in rural Florida, had ancestors who'd lived here.

Jimmy's head was hanging down, his gaze focused on the cell's cement floor.

"Did you call a lawyer?" I asked.

He shook his head without looking at me. "I didn't know who to call."

So he'd asked them to call me, a dog trainer. Just great!

"Can you pay a lawyer?"

His head came up. Then he cocked it to one side as if this was the first he'd thought about that. "Yeah. We'd gotten a line of credit on our house, to remodel the kitchen. I can use that for a lawyer."

"Okay, I'll try to find you a lawyer before I leave town. Where's your little girl?"

"I assume they took her to Sheila, but she's not that fond of dogs. I knew she wouldn't agree to take Buddy."

"Who's Sheila?"

"My sister-in-law." His face puckered up like he'd sucked on a lemon.

Did he and sister-in-law Sheila dislike each other, or was Jimmy assuming she too would turn on him?

Still, this Sheila might know who was the best lawyer in town. "What's her last name?"

"Collins."

My face must have shown my dismay because Jimmy grimaced and said, "Yeah, she's married to Julie's brother, the grandson of the town's founder."

He rubbed the back of his head and winced.

I twirled my finger in the air. "Turn around."

He complied. There was a knot the size of a golf ball on the back of his skull.

I blew out air. Maybe Jimmy Garrett wasn't being paranoid after all, and maybe, just maybe he hadn't killed his wife.

CHAPTER TWO

I plugged the address that the diminutive and sour-faced Doris had given me into my GPS, and it led me to a residential area a dozen blocks away from the sheriff's office. I parked across the street from a Cracker-style house, probably 1940s vintage, with clapboard siding, dormers in its peaked metal roof, and a large welcoming front porch. The Garretts had apparently been fixing it up. It sported a new paint job of off-white, with burgundy trim around the windows, and the small azaleas along the front had fresh dirt around them.

Unfortunately the recently planted bushes were taking a beating from the multiple official feet tramping around the yard. I stepped out of my car. There was surprisingly little chatter amongst the men and women moving around the front of the house. Most were grim-faced. I read that to mean they all knew, and probably liked, the victim.

I crossed the street to the line of sheriff's department cruisers and other vehicles parked randomly along the curb. As I walked past a plain gray car, I glanced down. A flash of red brought me up short. I looked again.

Buddy, in his red service animal vest, was sprawled across the backseat, his eyes closed, tongue hanging out of his mouth. The vehicle was otherwise unoccupied.

Anger and fear surged in my chest. What kind of idiot leaves a dog in a car in the intense Florida sun? Even in February, a closed car could turn into an oven in minutes.

I grabbed the door handle and yanked. It was locked, as was the front door. I banged on the window. "Buddy!"

The dog lifted his big black head, accented with tan Rottweiler markings above his eyes and under his chin.

I grabbed the door handle again as my knees wobbled from relief.

But his eyes didn't look right. They were glazed. He was definitely suffering. I had to get him out of that car, and fast.

I raced around to the other side and snatched at the door handles there. Both locked. The driver's window was cracked open a few inches. My blood boiled. Why did people think a cracked window was sufficient ventilation for an animal inside a car?

I managed to get my hand and my forearm in, but the elbow wouldn't fit. I maneuvered around, trying to find an angle that would allow me to reach down and unlock the door.

"What the heck do you think you're doing, young lady?"

I jumped, banging my elbow hard on the window frame. I tried to twist around to see who was behind me. I caught the profile of a tanned, rugged face under a cowboy hat just as searing pain shot up to my shoulder.

"Ow!" My elbow was now somehow inside the window and I couldn't get it out.

The man behind me made a harumphing noise. He lifted his hand and hit a button with his thumb. The car doors snicked unlocked.

He grabbed the door and started to open it.

More pain. "Yow! Stop!" My head swam.

"Okay, hold on." He grasped my upper arm with a surprisingly gentle hold. "Step back slowly as I open the door."

We performed an odd version of a two-step until there was room for his arm to reach in and hit the window button.

I extracted my arm and rubbed the sore elbow.

"I repeat, what the heck did you think you were doing?"

I rounded on the man. "What the heck was *I* doing? What were *you* thinking when you put that dog in a closed car?"

The man seemed unfazed by my raised voice. He took off his hat and ran fingers through sun-streaked brown hair before answering. "The window was cracked."

I glared at him. "That doesn't do much good. The sun can drive up the temperature inside a car to a hundred degrees or more, even this time of year."

Grrr. The jerk was smirking at me, his blue eyes lit with amusement.

He returned his hat to his head. "Didn't you notice the engine's running?"

Now that he'd pointed it out, I could indeed hear the soft purr of an engine. The bubble of anger in my chest deflated.

"Oh." Heat rose in my cheeks. "Well, why is he so listless?" Buddy had laid his head back down and closed his eyes.

"We had to tranquilize him. Jimmy was able to verbally control him, until we handcuffed him and put him in a car. Then the dog went nuts."

I narrowed my eyes. "He was only doing his job, protecting his human." Sheez, now I sounded like Mattie Jones.

"Look, I know that. You're his trainer, right?"

"Yeah." How had he figured that out? I could have been any animal lover passing by.

"Doris called me. Said to watch for a redhead with freckles."

"I don't have freckles," I automatically said, then remembered that I'd left the house without makeup, so indeed my freckles were showing. I was perversely pleased, however, that he thought I was a redhead.

"My hair's brown," I said. "The Florida sun gives it red highlights."

The man smiled for the first time, a big mouth full of pearly whites that had parts of my insides stirring. Parts that I'd been ignoring for several years.

That made me crabby. "What'd you tranq him with, an elephant gun?"

Despite my snotty tone, the man's smile didn't fade. "Nope, but you're close. One of our deputies has a friend with a gator farm. We called him in and he shot the dog with a dart, just a half dose. Said it was what he'd use on a baby gator."

"A gator farm?" Did every small town in central Florida have an outdated tourist trap?

"Yeah, he raises them to sell to zoos and restaurants."

I loved gator tail, that battered and deep-fried Florida specialty that you dip in a tangy sauce. But I'd never given much thought to where the gators came from.

"Alligators are a controlled species. Used to be endangered," the man volunteered, which only confused me more.

"Is it legal to raise them domestically then?"

He frowned. "Well, yeah."

For the first time I noticed his khaki shirt and the badge pinned to its pocket.

"Well, I guess you'd know, wouldn't you?" I laughed, then blushed again at the nervousness in my voice.

"He fishes them out of people's swimming pools too, for a small fee."

I squinted up into the deputy's face. The sun was now behind him, making it hard to see his features, but I thought I saw that teasing twinkle in his eyes again.

I pointed to the Stetson wannabe on his head. "You from Texas?"

"No. Upstate New York."

"Oh."

"Look, I didn't get to choose the uniform when I took office." Now he was frowning at me.

Way to go, Banks. Piss off law enforcement in a strange town.

"Uh, could I take the dog now?"

"Oh, sure." He opened the back door of the cruiser. "Come on, boy."

Buddy raised his head and looked at him, but made no other effort to move.

The deputy shook his head. "Hope I don't have to carry him. How much does he weigh?"

"About eighty pounds." I leaned over. "Come, Buddy." My tone brooked no disobedience.

Buddy struggled to his feet and took a step toward the door. He wobbled and I jumped forward, afraid he would tumble right out of the car.

The deputy crowded in next to me to help. I caught a whiff of woodsy aftershave and a hint of male sweat. He didn't seem to have any qualms about rolling *his* uniform sleeves up. The muscles in his arm rippled as he helped me assist Buddy out of the backseat and onto the road.

My pulse kicked up a notch. My insides stirred again.

Buddy shook himself, then staggered sideways two steps. I grabbed his collar, pulled a leash from my back pocket and clipped it on. But I hung onto the collar to steady him.

He stood still for a few seconds, legs splayed. Then he seemed to get his equilibrium back. Looking over his shoulder, he gave me a what's-up look. I'd forgotten that patented expression of his.

My heart swelled at the same time that my stomach sank. This poor dog might just have lost his human best friend.

Remembering my manners, I stuck out my right hand. "Thank you, Deputy…"

"Haines, ma'am. Will Haines."

He shook my hand with a firm grip. I appreciated it when a man did that, didn't go all limp just because he was shaking hands with a woman.

"Thanks, Deputy Haines."

"No problem." He touched his hat brim and turned away.

I was across the street and had Buddy stuffed halfway into my backseat when the words *when I took office* hit me.

I turned around and watched the scene across the street. Will Haines stood next to the cruisers at the curb. He gestured to another man in a khaki uniform who hurried over to him. They spoke for a few seconds, then Haines slapped the man on the shoulder. The guy took off, apparently to do Haines' bidding.

Crapola, Banks! He's the sheriff!

He must have sensed me watching him. He turned and sketched me another small salute.

I couldn't tell for sure from this distance but I suspected the smirk was back on his face.

I gave him a feeble wave, then ducked my head and scrambled around to the driver's side of my car.

CHAPTER THREE

I glanced frequently in the rearview mirror as I drove home. Buddy's condition had me worried. He was still glassy-eyed and apathetic. I wondered if I should take him to the emergency veterinarian hospital in Belleview, a town just south of Ocala that was a good bit bigger than Collinsville or Mayfair.

I was also contemplating the descriptions of Buddy's behavior. Jimmy woke up to find the dog standing over him growling, not letting the police get near. Buddy had been trained to bark for help should his handler become ill or fall, not try to keep potential help away. And why did he "go nuts" after they put Jimmy in a squad car? Had Jimmy neglected to give him the release command, the signal that let the dog know he was off duty? In the chaos of the situation, that was quite possible, but still "going nuts" was *not* how Buddy had been trained to behave.

I glanced again in the rearview mirror. He was now sleeping in the backseat, his limbs jerking sporadically in response to some dream.

Then again, the best of training might succumb to a dog's natural protective instincts when he'd just witnessed his owner kill his wife.

I shook my head. I didn't know that's what happened. Indeed, I was inclined to believe Jimmy's version, that he'd been struck from behind. Nonetheless, Buddy had witnessed violence, and he was now showing signs of being a traumatized dog.

By the time we arrived at my house, the tranquilizer had

apparently worn off. Buddy jumped out of the car under his own steam and seemed much more alert.

As I unlocked my front door, a deep woof came from one corner of the living room. That would be Max, the sixty-pound, tawny-colored rescue mutt of dubious parentage that I'd been training for several months now.

Then came a series of yaps from Lacy, a mostly-white bitch with at least one collie and an Alaskan husky or two amongst her ancestors.

Buddy looked at me. I nodded. He barked out a greeting.

Just one more woof from Max, but Lacy went bananas.

I shook my head. It looked like bringing a new dog into the house might set her back some.

One of the things I taught my dogs was to control their natural tendency to bark at anything that moved. Often people with PTSD were hypersensitive to sudden and/or loud noises. A dog yapping at things that weren't a threat was a problem for them.

Buddy still remembered that lesson, as did Max. But Lacy, not so much.

I sighed. Buddy and I stepped inside.

I fed the dogs and myself, let the dogs out back for a bathroom break, and then settled my trainees in their crates for the night. Buddy hadn't eaten much of the dinner I'd offered him. I didn't know if that was an aftereffect of the drug or a reaction to being uprooted from his home. Maybe some of both.

But he sniffed around the living room, then settled at my feet as I lounged on the sofa, sipping from a much needed glass of white wine and scrolling through my Netflix queue while waiting for the evening news to come on. I wanted to see how the media handled Julie's murder.

The living room was my favorite room in my little house. It was open and airy, with lots of windows that let the light in during the day. Even with dog crates in two corners, there was room for a small beige sofa, a matching armchair, and two end tables. The rug and the drapes, now pulled closed over the windows, were solid beige. The only accents in the room came from some throw pillows in bright red and turquoise (my favorite colors) and the pictures on the wall–a couple of prints of herons taking flight over a swamp.

The stone-faced fireplace didn't get much use during our short, mild winters, but it added a cozy feel to the room. Perched on its mantel was my only major indulgence, a forty-two inch, flat screen TV.

I glanced at my watch and clicked over to the news. No mention of Collinsville in the lead-ins on the Orlando stations. I jumped over to WCJB-20 out of Gainesville. Nothing there either. Collinsville was probably too far south to be considered local to them. After a bit more channel surfing, I found a Lakeland TV station.

And there was an image of Jimmy Garrett's house with a sheriff's department cruiser parked out front. A young female reporter stood in front of the dark house, describing the "grisly murder" by an Iraqi war veteran. "The sheriff's department has declined to comment, but a neighbor said Mr. Garrett suffers from post-traumatic stress disorder. His former boss reported that he has anger management problems."

Either the neighbor and the boss had declined to be interviewed on TV or that was all the time the station was willing to devote to a murder in a neighboring town. The news anchor flashed a toothy smile and switched to a human interest story about a local charity.

Poor Jimmy was being convicted by the press before he'd even been arraigned.

I clicked off the news and started closing up the house, turning out lights and checking locks.

Buddy looked around in confusion, as if it was just now occurring to him that he wasn't on some outing that would end with a trip back to his familiar home.

My chest aching, I tried to decide what to do. My trainees were always crated at night. But I only had two crates, and Buddy was used to sleeping beside his owner's bed. "Come on, boy. You're in my room."

First order of business the next day was to find a lawyer for Jimmy. It had been a restless night. Buddy had periodically stuck his head up over the side of my bed with a mournful look on his face. He was looking for Jimmy. The first couple of times, I fell right back to sleep after reassuring him with a pat on the head and a soft, "Lie down, boy." After the third time, he finally settled down, but I couldn't get back to sleep.

So now I was slurping down a second cup of coffee, while I did some computer research. The caffeine did its job, and I was a good bit more awake by the time I started making phone calls.

I scored on the third one. A law firm in Lakeland, Maher, Machaya and Kraft, promised to send an associate over to Collinsville to talk to Jimmy.

With that chore done, I turned my attention to the dogs. I really needed to get some training time in today, especially with Lacy. But first I wanted to do something to make Buddy feel better.

He's one of those dogs who likes taking a bath, so I dragged the big metal tub out into the backyard and filled it halfway with water from the garden hose. Leaving it in the bright sunlight to warm up a little, I went to get the rest of the bathing supplies.

As soon as I took Buddy out back, he realized what was up. He ran for the tub.

"Wait!" My universal stop-whatever-you're-doing-and-wait-for-instructions signal that I drummed into my dogs.

Buddy stopped beside the tub. I had some trouble getting his collar off. He was quivering all over with excitement but he waited until I'd removed it.

"Now, boy. Jump in."

I neglected to step back first and his enthusiastic entry into the tub soaked the front of my clothes. I managed to get him soaped up without too much additional soaking, then signaled for him to jump out of the tub so I could dump it and rinse him off.

He complied, his wet tail flapping back and forth, and I swear he was grinning at me. I flopped back on my butt, laughing.

I got him rinsed off, then quickly threw a big fluffy towel over him. Of course, he shook anyway, dislodging the towel and soaking me all over again.

I chuckled, then grabbed the towel and started roughly drying his silky black coat. "Welcome home, Buddy," I whispered in a damp, floppy ear.

Sadness overwhelmed me. I sank down on the grass again. I'd always been particularly fond of Buddy, partly because he was my first trainee and partly because he was just plain loveable. But when I'd delivered him to Jimmy, I'd been so excited about the success of my first training experience that the sadness of parting with the dog had been pushed aside.

Now I realized this could have no good outcome for me personally. If Jimmy was convicted, then my first big success as a trainer–or in my life in general for that matter–was a sham. If he was acquitted, I'd have to give up Buddy all over again.

Blinking back tears, I reached for the collar lying on the grass–a red strap stamped periodically in gold with the word *Marines*. "Come here, boy." I started to attach it around Buddy's neck, making a mental note to get him a new collar.

Stop that, Banks!

I shouldn't be trying to claim Buddy like that. It felt like I was wishing Jimmy was convicted. Not really the energy I wanted to put out into the universe.

I struggled to get the buckle fastened. Taking the collar back off, I examined it.

Firmly skewered on the buckle's prong was a small scrap of khaki-colored cloth.

CHAPTER FOUR

By the next morning, I realized I shouldn't have been so surprised by that piece of cloth. Someone from the sheriff's department had obviously snagged their uniform on the collar while wrestling the doped-up dog into the back of the sheriff's car.

I headed for the kitchen for some much needed caffeine, Buddy on my heels. Then suddenly he wasn't there.

I pivoted around. He'd darted back toward the bedrooms. Before I could follow to see what he was up to, he came back around the corner and dashed into the kitchen. A lump formed in my throat. He was looking for Jimmy.

Finally he stopped in the middle of the living room, tilted his head to one side and gave me his what's-going-on look.

"Sorry, boy," I managed to push past the lump.

Maybe a walk would be in order, before starting my morning training sessions. I intentionally did not put his service vest on, giving Buddy permission to just be a dog. He sniffed his way down my front sidewalk, marking my tiny front yard as his own, then we turned right.

Only three houses, one of them unoccupied, remained on my end of Main Street–the remnants of the section of town where the African-American laborers had once been segregated during the town's heyday.

Separating us from the Mayfair Motel were a couple of blocks of open fields, covered in wild palmettos, scraggly southern pines and the broken-down shells of other cottages–it doesn't take long for Florida's subtropical flora and fauna to retake unattended land.

Down the road, I spotted my friend, Edna Mayfair, walking her two black and white Spaniels. As usual, her gray hair was sticking up in all directions and her only concession to the weather was a dark sweater over her brightly colored muumuu. She returned my wave but kept going, back toward the motel. Several cars in its small parking lot told me she had guests to attend to.

At the motel, we turned the corner onto the only other major street in town, Mayfair Avenue. Clapboard Cracker houses, with low-peaked, metal roofs and spacious front porches, were scattered about. Near the far end of the street, close to where it connected with Highway 25, was a larger brick house, its two stories a rarity in Florida where second floors are hard to keep cool. Built to mimic the old plantation mansions, with tall white pillars supporting the veranda roof, it had been the pride and joy of old man Mayfair when he'd built it.

Now a young family owned it. The husband was some kind of technology geek who tele-commuted to his job in Atlanta.

His wife waved from the front yard, where she was playing with their two preschoolers. "New dog?" she called out.

I just nodded and bid her good morning, not in the mood to explain about Buddy.

I didn't get off so easy with my next-door neighbor, however.

My house was still the small, two-bedroom cottage it had always been. But the Wells' abode had been added on to through the decades. It resembled a train. The original house, the "locomotive," contained the main living spaces, with two "cars" of bedrooms cobbled onto its side and the "caboose" sunroom rounding the corner into the backyard.

Sherie Wells was standing on her porch as we approached. Even in a pale yellow terrycloth bathrobe, she was imposing.

She was around sixty but looked younger, partly because of her slim build and regal posture. Her mahogany skin was virtually wrinkle-free, except for tiny crow's feet beside her chocolate brown eyes. Shielding said eyes against the morning sun with one slender hand, she called out, "Mornin', Marcia. Isn't that Buddy?"

I was surprised she remembered him. It had been two years and several dogs ago when I'd been training him, but then again he'd been my first, and I had worked with him longer than subsequent trainees.

"Yes, ma'am." Although Mrs. Wells called me by my first name, I'd never gotten up the nerve to reciprocate. "His owner's having some issues right now, and I'm taking care of him temporarily."

She nodded. She was the quintessential nosy neighbor but she'd learned not to probe when it came to my clients. I was supposed to keep their backgrounds and issues confidential.

We chatted about the weather and her daughter's classes at the community college in Ocala, then I excused myself to get on with my day.

"May I pet him?" Mrs. Wells asked, holding out a hand, palm down, for him to sniff her fingers.

I hid a smile. I had her well trained. Looking down at Buddy, I nodded. "It's okay, boy."

Buddy wagged his tail and licked her hand. She bent down and petted him.

I was pleased to see the walk had cheered him up.

He helped with my morning training session with Lacy, setting her a good example as I tried to teach her to sit or stand facing backward whenever I stopped walking.

It's called the cover command. The service dogs literally "have the backs" of their humans. By watching what's going on behind them, the dogs help the PTSD sufferers be less anxious in public. No rapist, enemy soldier or other bad guy can sneak up on them.

After almost an hour of pacing up and down in the backyard, Lacy was finally turning around automatically two out of three times I stopped. Each time she did, I praised her verbally without turning around. If she continued to hold her position, I started walking again, and then gave her a treat from my pocket as she fell into step beside me.

Buddy's participation in the session had reminded me of Mattie's suggestion that I keep one of my trainees as a mentor dog for the others. I hadn't really been able to afford to do that before now, but maybe I would pick out a dog soon to train for that purpose. I wished I could keep sweet-tempered Max, but he was already committed to a client.

Indeed, I would need to schedule the training soon for his new owner, an Army medic who had done two tours in Afghanistan.

After lunch, I did a refresher session in the yard with Max. All of his skills were holding up nicely, even after several days of not receiving any reinforcement. He was definitely ready.

Still I put off calling his new owner to schedule the human phase of the training. I told myself that Lacy was at a fragile point and couldn't be ignored for days at a time while I was elsewhere, mentally and physically.

This was true, but I was also feeling too unsettled about the situation with Jimmy Garrett. I had heard nothing from him, his lawyer nor the sheriff's department. Of course, why should I expect to hear updates from any of them. I was only the dog-sitter after all.

When I opened the back door to let Max into the house, Buddy was standing just inside the door, looking lost and mournful. The effects of the walk had worn off already.

The pain in my chest told me that I'd never truly loved my ex-husband, because I hadn't felt this bad when we broke up. But now I knew what "heart-breaking" really felt like.

Without allowing time to talk myself out of it, I picked up my cell phone from its charger on the kitchen counter. Scanning recent calls gave me the Collinsville Sheriff's Department's number.

When Doris's slightly raspy voice answered, I asked for Sheriff Haines. I wasn't about to make my request of the unfriendly receptionist.

When she asked what I was calling about, I crisply said, "It's private."

A pause and then dead air. For a second, I thought she'd hung up on me.

Then that rugged male voice in my ear. "Haines."

"Sheriff, this is Marcia Banks."

"Who?"

I realized I'd never given him my name the other day. "The dog trainer who has Buddy."

"Oh yeah, yeah. What can I do for you, Ms. Banks?"

"I was wondering if it would be okay if I came to visit Jimmy?"

"Of course."

"And can I bring the dog?" I rushed the words out before he could say no. "He's been really down in the dumps. It would do him a world of good to see Jimmy."

The pause was slight. "I don't see why not. Jimmy's been pretty down too, understandably of course. Might do both of them good."

"Great. Can I come about four this afternoon?"

"Sure. If I'm not here, tell Doris I said it was okay."

I'd rather he told Doris it was okay, but decided not to say anything.

"Thanks so much."

I disconnected and looked down at Buddy. "We're going to see Jimmy, boy."

He tilted his head and gave a tentative wag of his tail.

At the sheriff's department, I turned over my purse, and Doris begrudgingly unlocked the door to let me into the inner sanctum. Buddy growled low in his throat as we passed her.

Say what?

That was out of character for him. I wondered if she had been one of the officers on the scene at Jimmy's the morning of Julie's death, when Buddy had valiantly tried to protect his unconscious human.

"You know where the cells are," Doris said, stepping back

over to the counter and putting her stool between Buddy and herself.

Once we were in the cell block, I unhooked Buddy's leash. He ran the last few steps.

"Buddy!" Jimmy yelled, hopping expertly across the cell toward us. He was now in an orange jumpsuit, with one leg pinned up. He patted the crossbar of the cell.

Buddy jumped up and joyously licked his human's face. Jimmy laughed and reached through the bars to scratch his ears.

I had assumed Jimmy was just taking a break from wearing his prosthesis, but when I looked around, it was nowhere in sight.

Jimmy must have noticed my perusal of the cell. "They took it away." His tone was offhanded as he continued to greet his dog.

Buddy's tail was wagging so hard, I feared he might fall over, since his front paws were still up against the bars.

"Settle, Buddy," Jimmy finally said. The dog dropped his front paws and tilted his head to one side. I couldn't see his face but I figured he was giving his human the what's-up look.

"Lie down, boy," Jimmy said.

Buddy dropped to the floor, then inched forward until he could get his nose through the bars and rest his chin on Jimmy's shoestringless sneaker. He gave me a sideways blissful glance.

I hated the thought of having to tear him away again. Maybe this hadn't been the best idea after all.

"So how are things going?" I asked.

Jimmy shrugged. "Could be better. The bank manager, who happens to be my brother-in-law, is refusing to let me draw on the home equity line of credit. Says it's in both mine and Julie's names so I can't use it until her estate is settled and I have clear title to the house."

My jaw dropped. "But that could be months."

"Yeah. Hey, thanks for finding that lawyer. He's a go-getter. Said he was going to check to see if it's legal for the bank to withhold that money. Oh and John's refusing me access to our joint bank accounts as well."

I presumed that John was Julie's brother, the bank manager. My blood boiled. Granted Jimmy was accused of killing his sister, but how unfair to prevent the man from being able to pay a lawyer.

"Even with the home equity loan," Jimmy said, "there won't be enough to cover my bond, so I'm stuck in here for now." He looked around the cell. "Prosecutor claimed I was a flight risk with quote, 'minimal ties to the community.'" Bitterness crept into his voice. "My lawyer pointed out that my daughter is hardly a minimal tie. But the judge set my bail at five-hundred thousand dollars anyway."

"How much would you have to put up for a bail bondsman?"

"Ten percent, and you don't get it back. That's all the money from the home equity line. And you have to put up collateral for the rest of it. I don't have anything worth that much."

"Ouch!"

"Yeah. I figured better to let the county give me free room and board so I can pay my attorney."

"That's good thinking," I said. "But I hate to see you have to be in here."

"Oh, it's not so bad. I just wish they'd get somebody besides Doris to bring me my meals. I wouldn't put it past her to spit in them before she comes down that hall."

I knew Jimmy was trying to put a good face on things, but I suspected he was miserable. Locked up like an animal, his wife dead, his child and dog taken away from him, and now they were making him hop around on one leg. Even if he proved his innocence eventually, this was bound to set back his recovery process.

"Is there a counselor I can call? Maybe he or she can come see you here."

"Nah, I stopped therapy last year. I was doing pretty good and we wanted to use the money for the home improvements we had planned…" His voice trailed off. Probably those improvements would never happen now. He'd be lucky to get any money out of the sale of the house, once he'd paid his lawyer.

I opened my mouth, then caught myself. I'd been about to

blurt out about the anger management problems. Was that real, or had his former boss made all that up to get his fifteen seconds of fame on the evening news?

My temper flared again. This whole thing was so unfair. Even if you're innocent, you end up broke. And how could they humiliate this man, this combat vet who had fought for all us, by taking his leg away?

I tried to cover up my anger, but the next question came out a little sharper than I'd intended. "Doesn't the VA provide free counseling?"

He ran a hand through his short hair. "Yeah, but the waiting list is as long as Main Street. I was gettin' a reduced rate, for bein' a vet and all, but it was still a fair amount out of our pockets."

I'd run out of things to say. "Hey, I'll try to get Buddy over to see you every few days."

Jimmy squatted down to the dog's level. "You don't have to do that. I know it's a long drive."

I was amazed he could balance like that on one foot.

"I want to," I said, "and besides Buddy misses you. I don't need a mopey dog around the house." I tried to chuckle but it came out sounding more like a stifled sob.

My hand was resting on one of the bars. Jimmy wrapped his long fingers around it and squeezed gently. "Thanks for everything, Marcia. You're an angel."

I snorted.

"Seriously, thanks for believing in me." His eyes were shiny. "Especially since nobody else around here seems to."

"Hey, Buddy's a good judge of character. Since he likes you, that's good enough for me." It was an inane thing to say, but it was all I could come up with.

We exchanged goodbyes.

Once around the corner, I marched down the hall and right up to Doris. Buddy growled low in his throat.

I stared down at him for a beat, then decided to let it slide. After all he'd had a rough couple of days.

"Where's Sheriff Haines?" I demanded.

Doris had jumped off her stool. She put it between herself and the dog. "Uh, he's in his office."

"Where's that?"

She gestured past the couple of paper-strewn desks behind her to a closed door. "But you can't take that mutt in there." She hadn't taken her eyes off Buddy during the whole exchange.

"Fine. I'll leave him here with you then."

Her head jerked up.

I gave her a fake smile, my eyes boring into hers.

She shook her head vehemently.

I shortened Buddy's leash. He wasn't wearing his service dog vest but he got the message. He stood up straight and stayed right by my side as I marched past the empty desks to the faux wooden door at the back of the room.

I debated for a second, then knocked. It probably wouldn't win me any points if I barged in on the man.

"Come in."

I opened the door. "I need to talk to you for a minute."

He made a come-ahead gesture with his hand and stood up as I stepped into his office.

Without the sun in my eyes, I had a much better view of the man. Based on his rugged face I would have put him in his forties, but when he flashed his pearly whites, as he was now, he looked younger. His broad shoulders nicely filled his khaki uniform shirt.

Once again his sleeves were rolled up even though today's temperature was the more normal low seventies of February. The hair on his arms was bleached almost white against his tan.

"Ms. Banks. Good to see you. Did you visit with Jimmy yet?"

His words pulled me away from my study of his muscular arms and reminded me I was angry. I put my hands on my hips, inadvertently tugging on Buddy's leash. He tilted his head up at me.

"I want to know why you all took Jimmy's prosthesis away from him."

The sheriff's face sobered. "One of the deputies pointed out that he could use it as a weapon against us."

"Which deputy?" My bet was on Doris.

He narrowed his eyes at me. "It doesn't matter. It was a good point. That thing would make a formidable club."

"You can't do this to him, Sheriff. It's humiliating to have to hop around like…like a cripple." I couldn't think of a more politically correct word.

The sheriff grimaced. "I know. I don't like it. But it's my job to protect my deputies, and also my prisoners, from harm. He could conceivably use that thing to hurt himself as well."

"How? By beating himself over the head with it? Speaking of which," I said through gritted teeth, "did you see the lump on the back of his head the day Julie was killed?"

"Yeah. He said somebody hit him from behind when he came in the door, knocked him out."

"And that's so hard to believe, considering the lump?"

"He might've hit his head on something when he fell down. There's a heavy piece of furniture next to the door." He held his hands wide apart to indicate a large object. "One of those big credenza things."

"*Maaybe…*" I dragged the word out, "the killer hit him with something heavy and then took it with him. *Maybe* it was the murder weapon. Julie might have interrupted a burglary." I was talking fast now, spitting mad. "And Jimmy says he wasn't drinking. He'd been out running with Buddy, stopped at the park. Surely someone saw him."

The sheriff's eyes had gone hard. His lips were pressed together. "I can't remember the last time we had a burglary around here. Most folks don't even lock their doors."

Arrgh! This man was, was impossible. And smug. I hated smug men.

"The 'murder weapon,'" he made air quotes, "was a metal radiator. Jimmy–" He stopped and took a deep breath, obviously trying to calm himself. "Whoever killed Julie bashed her head against it."

I winced and dropped into his visitor's chair. Suddenly I didn't feel so good. Buddy settled his rump on the floor beside me.

The sheriff also resumed his seat. "Of course, Jimmy says he wasn't drinking, but he stank of beer. And no, nobody saw him that morning, at least not during the time of death window."

"And how hard would it be for the same person who conked him on the head to pour a beer over him while he lay there unconscious?"

"Not very, but where did the beer come from?"

That stopped me for a moment. Jimmy said he'd stopped drinking completely months ago, so it was unlikely the Garretts' fridge had any beer in it. And most people didn't carry a beer can around in their back pocket at nine in the morning.

"So there was no beer in the house?"

He shook his head. "And before you ask, no empties either. For which I have no good explanation."

"Did you test Jimmy's blood alcohol level?"

"He wouldn't let us."

That stopped me again. Couldn't the police make you take such a test if you were thought to have committed murder while in a drunken rage? And Jimmy's refusal to allow the test didn't jive with his claims of innocence.

The sheriff combed fingers through his sun-streaked hair. "By the time I got a court order and did the test, his blood alcohol level was normal."

"How long after the…" I winced again, "…you know, was that?"

"Three hours. As you will recall, I was tied up for a while dealing with an out-of-control dog who wouldn't let us into the crime scene."

"Oh come on!" I started to throw up my arms, but remembered at the last second that one was attached to Buddy's leash. I settled for a one-arm gesture. "You think Jimmy was drunk enough to kill his wife and then pass out, and three hours later his alcohol level is normal?"

"No, I think he was drunk enough to lose control of his temper and bash his wife's head in, then stagger out into the living room, maybe in shock over what he'd just done, and maybe trip over his own feet and hit his head on the way down."

He held his hand out toward me. "Look, I don't know for sure that Jimmy killed his wife, but the evidence pointed his way so I arrested him. The prosecutor presented his case and the judge bound him over for trial."

"And your job is done." My voice dripped sarcasm.

He blew out air. "Yes and no. I'm still checking things out, tying up loose ends."

"So you can hang Jimmy."

"No, so I'm sure we've gotten to the truth of the matter," he said through gritted teeth.

My mother's voice in the back of my head was telling me to be nice.

I ignored her and changed tactics. "Who put the dog in your car?"

His eyes registered surprise. "I did."

"Did anybody else handle him before that?"

"No. After we loaded Jimmy into one of the cars, the dog stood on the front porch and wouldn't let us get near the house. Not until the tranquilizer dart started to take effect. Then I led him to my car, locked him in so nobody would mess with him. *And* turned on the engine and the air conditioner."

Heat rose in my cheeks at the reminder of my embarrassing assumptions that morning. But I opted to ignore that too.

"Were your sleeves rolled up then?"

"When? That morning? Yeah, probably. I wear them this way most of the time. I hate long sleeves, but I didn't get to choose–"

"The uniform when you took office," I said.

He actually gave me a small smile, which pissed me off all over again.

"Why the third degree?" he asked.

"I found a piece of khaki cloth caught in the buckle of Buddy's collar the next day."

The sheriff seemed to ponder that information for a moment, then he shrugged. "There are a lot of plausible explanations for that."

I already knew that but I perversely said, "Such as?"

He shrugged again. "Maybe Jimmy or Julie own something khaki. It's not a color limited to my department's uniforms."

"Would you check their closets?"

The man gave me an annoyed look. "Why?"

I didn't have a good answer for that. I knew I was grasping at straws. So I went for snark, always my best weapon. Imitating his deep voice, I said, "So we're sure we've gotten to the truth of the matter."

He stood and started around the end of his desk. Buddy quickly moved to put himself between us, as he'd been trained to do, but his tail was wagging slightly.

The sheriff stopped. "Thank you for coming in, Ms. Banks. I appreciate your input, and I can assure you I am looking into all aspects of the situation." He sounded like he was practicing his sound bite for the evening news.

I decided it was probably not good timing to ask if I could bring Buddy to see his owner again in a few days. Maybe I'd just show up and take my chances that they wouldn't turn us away.

I rose from my chair. "Thank you for seeing me." My tone was equally formal. I turned on my heel and sashayed out of his office, dog in tow. I was halfway across the empty bullpen when I heard the sheriff's loud and exasperated sigh.

Part of me wanted to throw some biting comment back over my shoulder, if I could only think of one. Another part couldn't blame him for being annoyed with me. I really needed to learn to control my temper better.

You get more bees with honey than with vinegar. My mother's voice in my head.

"Aw, shut up, Ma," I muttered under my breath as Buddy and

I exited the police station. Then I instantly felt guilty for being rude to my mother, if only in my imagination.

I looked down at Buddy. He wagged his tail.

At least this visit had improved one of our moods.

CHAPTER FIVE

Buddy definitely seemed in better spirits the next day. He still did his search-the-rooms-for-Jimmy routine a couple of times that morning, but he wasn't as mopey.

The day was unseasonably warm and after my morning training session with Lacy, I came inside a bit sweaty and quite thirsty. I crated Lacy and gave Buddy the off-duty signal–hands crossed in front at the wrists, then spread apart, then crossed again–a gesture no one is likely to make accidentally.

I was standing at the kitchen sink, swigging down a cold bottle of water, when a familiar voice called out, "Knock, knock."

Buddy let out one sharp bark and tore in the direction of the voice.

"Wait!" I wasn't sure if he would remember Becky.

But he did. He stood in the kitchen doorway, looking into the living room, his ears perked and his whole body quivering.

"Okay, boy." He took off.

When I got to the door, Becky was stooped down, scratching Buddy's ears and receiving doggy kisses.

I laughed. "You're a bad influence, Beck."

She shook her head, dark curls bouncing around her heart-shaped face. She tried for a solemn expression but failed miserably. "People have been telling me that since I was six."

"Ah, so you were a late bloomer."

Becky smirked and stood up. "You got another one of those?" She pointed to the water bottle in my hand.

"Sure. I was about to fix myself some lunch. Want some?"

"I thought you'd never ask. I'm starved!"

"So what brings you to this neck of the woods?" I said over my shoulder as I headed back to the kitchen.

Becky trailed after me, smelling of eucalyptus and shea butter, the snug-fitting bodice of her blue cotton dress showing off her curvy figure, the skirt swirling loosely around her shapely legs. I stifled an all-too-familiar spurt of envy.

"In-home massage with a movie star," she said.

"John Travolta?" He was the most prominent of the celebrities who had estates scattered throughout the horse country surrounding Ocala.

I tossed Becky a water bottle, then gathered whole grain bread, cheese, tomatoes and mayo on the counter. I'd intended to make tuna salad, but Becky was a vegetarian so I opted to go meatless today as well.

"Nah, this guy's not that big yet." Becky swiped a corner off a slice of cheese. "And I'm not supposed to tell people his name. He's trying to keep a low profile."

I smiled, pleased that Becky's massage therapy practice was thriving. When I'd first moved down here, she and I were neighbors in a low-rent apartment complex in Ocala. We both got out of there as fast as possible, me to my little house in Mayfair and she to a studio apartment that had once been the owner's oversized garage. But by the time we'd vacated the Armpit Apartments (Becky's name for them, not their real moniker), we were fast friends.

"Hey, I did try to call first," she said. "But it went to voicemail. Figured I'd take a chance and stop by anyway, since I was already nearby."

I'd wondered about that. Becky was the only person I trusted with a key to my house, but she knew better than to pop in unannounced, lest she interrupt a training session. Then again, I did most of the training in the backyard. If I hadn't been inside, she would have made herself at home until I came in.

I pulled my cell phone out of my pocket. I hadn't felt it vibrate. Then I realized why. The dang thing had run out of juice. I tossed it on the counter to charge later.

I grabbed the plates with the sandwiches I'd made. "Come on. Let's sit outside."

"Sure. You got any sweet tea?"

I made a face at her and turned to push the kitchen screen door open with my butt.

"Pitcher of unsweetened is in the fridge. Grab the sugar bowl from the table, and some napkins."

We settled at the tiny bistro table on my equally tiny back deck. She doctored her iced tea, then made as if she was going to put a whole teaspoon of sugar in mine. Knowing the move was coming, I deftly blocked her.

The iced tea controversy was a source of continued friendly banter between us, with Becky insisting you couldn't call yourself a true Floridian until you developed a taste for iced tea so sweet it made your teeth ache. On this issue, I planned to stay a staunch Northerner, partly because I didn't need the extra calories. They would go straight to my hips.

We ate in silence for a couple of minutes. Then Becky said, "So why is Buddy visiting with you today?"

I grimaced around a mouthful of sandwich, then took a swig of just-barely-sweetened iced tea to wash it down. "His owner's in jail."

Becky's mouth fell open.

I wasn't allowed to talk about specific symptoms or anything that identified my clients, but I figured police records were public so I filled her in, without mentioning names.

"Wow." She sat back in her chair, eyes wide. "Do you think he did it?"

"I don't know," came out of my mouth, but I was shaking my head.

"Who else could have done it? Don't those vets often have a lot of anger issues?"

My own temper flared. "Not always," I said, trying to keep my voice neutral.

Becky held her hands up, palms out. "Sorry. I said *often*, not always." She picked up a half sandwich from her plate. "Hey, was Buddy there, you know, when it happened?"

Lacy had crawled into her crate for a well-deserved snooze after her training session, but Max and Buddy lay at our feet on the deck. Buddy raised his head at the mention of his name.

"Yeah," I said. "He was there."

"Then he knows who the killer is."

While we finished our lunch, I pondered Becky's comment. Buddy had growled at Doris at the police station. Did that mean anything?

My Thursday didn't go as planned. I didn't get down to visit Jimmy. So I decided to make the trip a priority the next day. After a quick morning session with Lacy, I put her and Max in their crates with plenty of water, made myself a PBJ to eat along the way and headed out.

I buzzed along the country roads between Mayfair and Collinsville, with Buddy in his service dog vest in the backseat. I was still trying to decide if I should have called first. It was a long drive to make if we weren't going to get in to see Jimmy. But it would also be too easy for that Doris person to say no if I called. And after my little pissing match with the sheriff on Tuesday, I wasn't sure how receptive he would be either. I was hoping Southern manners would take over if I was standing in front of them.

That didn't happen with Doris. "You can't just waltz in here whenever you please."

A soft growl rumbled low in Buddy's throat.

I flashed back to Becky's comment.

Could Doris be the killer?

I'd put Buddy's vest on him today with the intention of reinforcing his training. He was currently in the cover position, standing next to me at the counter but facing behind me.

I dangled my left hand down, turning my palm toward his face. He touched the palm with his nose. It was the most basic signal, essentially a nonverbal "hey, pay attention." It served as a reminder that he was working.

Had Doris always disliked Jimmy, or was she just assuming he'd killed Julie? If Buddy had picked up on animosity between Doris and his owner during previous encounters, that wouldn't have endeared her to him.

Still, he shouldn't be breaking training like this.

The whoosh of the station's outer door opening behind me and the scuff of shoes on tile.

Buddy alerted me to the person's presence with a thump of his tail, but when I glanced down the hair along his back was standing straight up. I detected another soft rumble in his throat.

I glanced over my shoulder. A male deputy had entered the lobby. Putting my hand on Buddy's head, I said in a low voice, "Settle down."

Okay, so much for the growling being a clue to the murderer. The dog was no doubt reacting to the khaki uniforms, associating them with the people who had hauled his owner away, and then had tried to invade his home.

The deputy was fortyish, a beefy guy, about six-two and at least two hundred, forty pounds. I pegged him as a former high-school football player who was now slowly going to fat.

"What's the problem, Doris?" He took a swaggering step toward me.

Buddy inserted himself between us, as he'd been trained to do.

"Friend," I said softly, but Buddy's body did not relax. I told him to sit. He complied and gave me his patented tilt of the head.

Doris answered the deputy in the same snippy tone she'd used with me. "Ain't nothin' you need to worry about, Frank."

Did this woman like anybody?

Frank blinked a couple of times, probably trying to figure out how to save face.

I flashed him my most charming smile. "This is Jimmy Garrett's service dog. He's been pining for his owner so I brought him for a visit."

Frank returned my smile and stepped over to push the door to the inner sanctum open. It didn't budge. "Hit the buzzer, Doris."

Doris let out an exaggerated sigh. "I already told her no. We can't have people just waltzin' in here any old time."

"I'll come during your regular visiting hours in the future, but it's a long drive from my house. Since I'm already here…" I let my voice trail off and smiled at Frank again.

"We don't have regular visitin' hours," he said. "Don't usually got prisoners in jail long enough for it to matter."

"So I don't quite understand then…" I trailed off again, trying to play the confused female, not my best role.

"Come on, Doris. Let her go back there. How can it hurt?"

Doris frowned at him, then turned her pinched look on me. "Ten minutes." She held out her hand for my purse and I gave it to her. The buzzer sounded.

I kept Buddy on the other side of me as we went through the door that Deputy Frank held open for us. Normally, I'd trust his training not to bite people, even those he doesn't like, but he'd been acting out of character lately. And now would not be the best time for him to take a chunk of khaki out of a pants' leg.

Jimmy's greeting lacked some of the enthusiasm of the last visit. He looked a bit bedraggled, his face stubbled, his skin grayish under his tan. The garish orange jumpsuit didn't help. I doubted it was complementary to anyone's complexion.

It took a moment to register that he was walking normally. Apparently my pissing match with the sheriff had not been for naught. He had his prosthesis back.

I signaled to Buddy that he was off duty, and Jimmy crouched down beside the bars. Human and dog exchanged ear scratches for face licks.

Then Jimmy stood up. Buddy pushed his head under Jimmy's hand, his tail still going a mile a minute.

Jimmy's eyes were dull and lifeless. "Thanks for coming, Marcia. It's good to see a friendly face for a change."

Alarm tightened my chest. "Is anybody mistreating you?"

A hesitation so slight I wondered if I'd imagined it. "No. Doris just scowls a lot. The others are…" He trailed off and looked away.

Unfortunately Doris was the one he probably interacted with the most. While we were on the subject, I figured I might as well dig a little. "Has she always disliked you?"

He shook his head. "Doris don't truly like many people, but Julie was one of them. They were good friends. So I can see why she's soured on me now, since she and pretty much the whole town are sure I did it."

His despondent tone made my throat ache. "Did Julie have any enemies?"

"Not really. She and our next-door neighbor got into it a couple a times. Miss Shirley tends to be a gossip, and that drove Julie nuts."

I wasn't sure how to broach the next topic, so I just blurted out my question. "Uh, why didn't you let the sheriff's department do a sobriety test that morning?"

He gave me a blank look. After a moment, he shook his head. "I was crazy out of my mind at first with grief. Not feelin' all that cooperative. I don't even remember them askin' me."

That was plausible, and if Jimmy was lying, he was one heck of a good actor.

He dropped his gaze down to Buddy, absentmindedly scratching behind his ears. Buddy looked like he was going to swoon. But Jimmy couldn't have looked more forlorn if he'd tried.

I was seriously worried about his mental health. "Hey, what's the name of that counselor you used to go to?"

He narrowed his eyes at me. "I don't have any money to pay her. Besides there ain't nothin' she can do about all this." He waved a hand to encompass his cell.

"No, I was going to refer a friend to her," I ad-libbed, "but if she isn't that great…" I was getting pretty good at this trailing off thing.

His face lit up some. "No, no, she's fantastic. Really helped me a lot. Her name's Jo Ann Hamilton. She's in Lakeland."

"Thanks." I repeated the name in my head a couple of times so I wouldn't forget it.

Then it occurred to me that if Doris and Julie were good friends, she would have been around Buddy a fair amount. "Hey, has Doris always been afraid of dogs?"

Jimmy's eyebrows arched up. "No, not at all."

"That's funny. She and Buddy don't seem to like each other."

"Really? They've always gotten along fine."

Hmm, interesting. So why was Buddy now growling at her? It could be a generalized reaction to khaki uniforms, although he hadn't reacted negatively to the sheriff.

More importantly, why was Doris now afraid of him?

Jimmy and I chatted awkwardly for a few more minutes. It's hard to make small talk with a man behind bars. Finally I figured we'd stayed long enough.

"Well, I'd better be getting back."

Jimmy squatted down to say his goodbyes to Buddy.

I wanted to promise to keep coming to visit, but I wasn't sure how much longer I'd be able to fit it into my schedule, especially since I really needed to start working with Max's new owner soon. My stomach clenched and my throat hurt. But still I resisted making a promise I wasn't sure I could keep. I settled for, "I'll try to bring Buddy by when I can."

Jimmy just nodded, still crouched down. He gave Buddy one final pat on the head, and then stood up. His eyes were shiny. "You take good care of him, Marcia."

My throat closed completely. I swallowed hard. "You know I will."

He nodded again and turned away.

My eyes stung.

"Thanks for bringing him," he mumbled, his back to me, his

voice sounding a little choked up.

I suspected he was fighting tears. I wanted to get out of there before he lost the battle, which would no doubt get me blubbering as well and would embarrass both of us.

But Buddy was resisting leaving. He whined softly.

"Come on, boy." The dog followed me out, but he kept looking back over his shoulder.

Once we were on the sidewalk, I rummaged in my purse for my cell phone, intending to look up the number for the counselor and give her a call. I doubted this Jo Ann Hamilton would be willing to drive over from Lakeland to see Jimmy for free, but I wanted her to know what was going on. And I wanted to ask her about his so-called anger management issues.

After practically turning my purse inside out, I realized my phone was not in there.

Crapola!

I visualized it lying on my kitchen counter, waiting to be recharged. How many calls had I missed in the last two days?

I turned around and went back into the sheriff's department building. "Can I use your phone for a minute?"

"No," Doris said.

I took a deep breath, counted to five. "Could I speak to the sheriff, please?"

"He's at lunch."

I couldn't think of anything to say to that, so I turned on my heel and marched out again.

Buddy looked up at me and tilted his head.

I scratched his nearest ear. "I guess human beings seem quite strange to you sometimes, eh boy."

We started for my car. Then I noticed the sign over one of the storefronts on Main Street and detoured in that direction. If the sheriff was at lunch, it was a good bet he was inside the diner.

I stepped inside the door with Buddy beside me.

"Hey, you cain't bring that dog in here." The voice came from a woman of Romanesque proportions stuffed into a waitress uniform at least one size too small. All she needed was chewing gum to complete the stereotype. She was marching toward us.

Buddy stepped between us. I pointed to his red vest. "He's a service dog."

"So what? Health department regs say no animals in eating establishments." She dragged out the last word, emphasizing each syllable.

"So service dogs are allowed. They're the exception."

"Not in my diner, they ain't."

"Then you're in violation of the law."

She looked me up and down. "What you need a service dog for anyway? You look able-bodied enough to me."

"And that question is *also* in violation of the law," I pushed through gritted teeth. "You're not allowed to ask me why I have a service animal."

"Aw, that's so much BS. It don't take nothin' ta have a critter labeled as a service animal in this state."

Although what she said was true–it was ridiculously easy to get a service animal designation in Florida–that did not change the fact that she had to let Buddy come into the diner, no questions asked. Normally I might have let it slide but the woman's ignorance and her attitude had me completely riled.

"Jane, it's okay," a deep voice rumbled.

I leaned to one side to peer past the woman. Sheriff Haines was sitting alone in a booth about halfway back on the right side.

"She's right," he said. "Let her come in." He waggled his fingers at me in a come-here gesture.

"Harumph." Jane pivoted around far more gracefully than I would have thought possible and stomped away.

I led Buddy to the sheriff's booth and told him to lie down. He complied, wiggling in some under the table and settling in front of my feet as I sat down on the bench opposite the sheriff.

"You want something? Coffee? A sandwich?"

"No thanks. I had lunch." Although I was regretting the PBJ. The meatloaf on the sheriff's plate looked really good, and it smelled even better. "Uh, coffee would be nice."

He looked around, but Jane had made herself scarce.

The sheriff patted his mouth with his napkin, then stood up. "Be right back."

I thought about telling him never mind. I really didn't want to deal with Jane again.

But he didn't go looking for the woman. Instead he leaned over the lunch counter and stretched his arm toward the coffee maker on a ledge behind it. His fingers curled around the handle of the glass carafe on its burner. He looked back over his shoulder. "High test or decaf?"

I smiled. "Definitely high test."

He nabbed a white china mug from a tray on the counter and brought both the mug and coffee pot over to the booth. "You need cream?"

"Nope, black is fine."

He poured coffee into the mug, topped off his own cup, then returned the pot to its burner behind the counter.

When he resumed his seat, I asked, "So why are you the only one in this town who acts normal?"

"What do you mean?"

I was already regretting blurting that out. I didn't want to complain about Deputy Doris. Not the best way to keep on the good side of a lawman, to dis his people.

I shrugged. "Let's just say the red carpet around here is more a dark shade of brown."

He laughed, a pleasant chuckle that made me feel funny inside.

Heat crept up my face. I focused on my mug, picking up a nearby spoon and vigorously stirring the coffee in it.

"You don't usually see people stir black coffee," he said conversationally.

I pulled the spoon out of the cup and dropped it on the table. Now my cheeks were burning up. I cleared my throat and opted to act like nothing had happened.

Because indeed, nothing *had* happened, so why was I blushing?

"Thanks for giving Jimmy's prosthesis back to him."

"No problem. He and I had a chat. He promised not to use it as a weapon. I believe he's a man of his word."

I bit back the first retort that came to mind. *Then why don't you believe him when he says he's innocent?*

Of course, it wasn't about what the sheriff believed, it was about what evidence pointed to what. And I honestly wasn't one hundred percent sure *I* believed Jimmy was innocent.

"Uh, where did Jimmy work?"

The sheriff paused with a forkful of meatloaf halfway to his mouth. "He hasn't worked in a while. He was taking care of their baby." He shoveled the food into his mouth and chewed. Once he'd swallowed, he added, "Except he did work part-time for a few months after they moved here."

"Where?"

"Down at the hardware store."

I nodded, having decided that I wanted to check out the ex-boss's comment about anger issues before leaving town. I took a sip of coffee, trying to appear nonchalant. "Do you know why he stopped working there?"

The sheriff shrugged. "Nobody works for old man Kroger very long."

"What do you mean?"

"Let's just say he's not an easy man to deal with."

"Can I ask you a question?"

He arched an eyebrow at me, the corners of his mouth quirking upward. "I thought you just did. Several, in fact."

"Another question then."

"Shoot."

"How did you know to go to Jimmy's house that morning?"

The sheriff was chewing again. He hastily swallowed. "Anonymous phone call. Person said the Garrett's door was sitting open and a dog was barking inside."

"Wasn't there a name and number on caller ID? Who took the call?"

He'd shoveled some mashed potatoes and gravy into his mouth. He took a swig of coffee to wash it down. "Doris. She said the caller ID info was blocked."

"Did she recognize the voice?" I found it hard to believe in a town this size that she wouldn't.

"She said she didn't, but I figured it was the Garrett's neighbor, Miss Shirley."

"And when you got there, Jimmy was still lying on the floor, out cold?"

"No. He was on the floor, but he was groggy. The dog was standing over him, barking like crazy." The sheriff ducked his head to one side and looked at Buddy under the table. "Hard to believe it's the same dog."

Defensive anger surged in my chest. "He was doing what he's been trained to do, barking to summon help if something happens to Jimmy."

"So why wouldn't he let us get near Jimmy until the man came around enough to tell him to settle down?"

The question took me by surprise. It was a very good one, and I had no answer. So I just shrugged.

The sheriff picked up his plate, now empty except for a few scraps of meatloaf and smears of gravy, and leaned down to set it on the floor. "Here, Buddy."

The dog rustled against my feet but made no move toward the plate. Service dogs are valuable animals. It wouldn't be good to have them get sick from eating something tainted, so they're trained not to eat anything that isn't approved by their handlers.

Sheriff Haines gave me a funny look. "Doesn't he like meatloaf?"

"He won't touch it unless I tell him it's okay."

The sheriff looked impressed. "So tell him."

"I think not." I'd just caught sight of Jane barreling toward us from the back of the diner.

"Will Haines, you'd better not be lettin' that mutt lick my plates!"

CHAPTER SIX

It didn't take long for me to discover what the sheriff had meant regarding "old man Kroger."

Once again I was greeted at the door with, "You cain't bring that dog in here."

I swallowed a sigh. "He's a service dog."

The old codger standing in my path was maybe two inches taller than me, which made him downright short for a man, since I'm only five-five in flats. But he was brandishing a broom like a weapon, which made him a bit more formidable. I wasn't in the mood to get whacked in the head with a wooden handle.

Buddy inserted himself between me and the threat. Unwilling to use the term *friend* regarding a grumpy little man shaking a broom at me, I used the palm touch signal instead to let Buddy know it was okay. To Mr. Kroger, I said, "You can't bar service animals from a place of business."

Then I got a better look at the store, and I wasn't so sure *I* wanted to go inside. Dust motes danced in the sunlight streaming through the open door. The aisles were narrow and the shelves dusty.

A tall, teenaged boy appeared behind the store owner. Too-long, dirty blond hair fell across a pimply forehead, creating a veil over pale blue eyes. The kid's mouth was set in a grim line. "You want me to sweep or not, Mr. Kroger?" He put his hand on the broom handle, above the old man's head.

Begrudgingly, Mr. Kroger relinquished the broom. The young

man gave me a shy smile before turning away.

I silently blessed my rescuer.

"And what are you smirkin' at, young lady?" the old man said.

"Nothing. I only wanted to ask you a couple questions."

"'Bout what?"

"About when Jimmy Garrett worked here."

"That jack… uh, jerk." He might be a grouchy old codger but he was clearly raised in an era when men didn't curse in front of women.

I decided to cut to the chase. I didn't particularly want to be in this man's company any longer than necessary. "Were you the former employer they interviewed for the TV news a few days ago?"

The man stood up straighter and smiled a little at the mention of his fifteen seconds of fame. "Yeah."

"You said Jimmy has anger management problems. On what are you basing that statement?"

He narrowed his eyes. "You a lawyer?"

"No. I train service animals."

He looked down at Buddy. "Hey, ain't that Jimmy's dog?"

"Yes, I'm taking care of him for now."

The man smiled. It was not a pretty sight. "You sweet on him, like those gals on that TV show, what fall in love with criminals in prison?"

This time I didn't bother to stifle the sigh. "No. I only wanted to know what you meant by anger management problems."

"Well, he jest blew up at me one day, and up and quit."

"Blew up at you how?"

"He said I was worse than the meanest drill sergeant and he stomped out."

"He said it. He didn't yell it?"

The man opened his mouth, then closed it again. "Well, I don't recall. I think he might've yelled it."

"Sheez, and on that you based the assumption that he has problems controlling his anger?"

"Well, he done killed his wife, didn't he? Bashed her head

in, I heard."

I ground my teeth. "No, *someone* bashed her head in. Jimmy is innocent until proven guilty."

Then I realized how futile this conversation was. This old man wasn't going to change his mind, and his opinion really didn't matter. Jimmy's attorney would be able to make him look like the fool that he was, should the local prosecutor be dumb enough to put the man on the witness stand at Jimmy's trial.

"Thanks for your time, Mr. Kroger." I turned and left the store.

I walked slowly toward my car, processing. Deciding really. I had a bad feeling Jimmy wasn't going to survive months in jail with his sanity intact.

Buddy stepped across in front of me just as a shadow fell across my path. I jerked a little.

The teenager from Kroger's Hardware was standing in front of us on the sidewalk.

"It's okay, boy," I said. "Friend."

The kid was still holding the broom. "Mr. Kroger's full of crap, ma'am. Everybody who's ever worked for him ends up quitting, and some have done so a lot noisier than Jimmy did."

I squinted to look up at him. The sun was behind him. "I'd figured that out, but thanks for verifying it. Would you be willing to testify to that effect, if needed, at Jimmy's trial?"

He shuffled his feet. "I guess so. But my folks, they think Jimmy's guilty."

"What do you think?"

"I think we shouldn't be judgin' him until he's been tried. Like you said, innocent until proven guilty."

"Then your folks have raised you right. I'd imagine they'd expect you to tell the truth?"

"Oh, yes, ma'am."

"Then regardless of how they feel about Jimmy, they shouldn't object to you testifying and telling what you know to be true."

He shuffled his feet again. "No ma'am. I guess not." Then he grinned at me. "I better get back. I'm tryin' to stick it out long enough to buy my girlfriend a nice birthday present."

I returned his smile. "She's a lucky girl."

He ducked his head. "Thank you, ma'am."

"Boy, what are you doin' out there?" the old man yelled from the store entrance behind me.

"Comin', Mr. Kroger." The kid took off.

Later I would blame it on the long drive home. It gave me too much time to think, too much time to work up a good sense of outrage over the attitudes of the people in Collinsville.

During the last two years, I'd worked with a dozen veterans. They came from various branches of the military and had seen action in various parts of the world, but the one thing they had in common was their PTSD. They'd developed this debilitating syndrome while serving their country, protecting the rights and freedom of the rest of us who continued to lead our cozy lives back home.

Then they came back to the states, and sometimes they got what they needed from the Veterans Administration, and sometimes they didn't. A prosthesis for a physical injury, yes, but getting a service animal to help with the psychological symptoms, that was a different story.

The not-for-profit agency I worked for provided the animals at the lowest cost possible, and even then they had scholarships for vets who couldn't afford the ten-thousand dollar fee. If I could, I'd train the animals for free, but I have to eat and pay my bills. As it is, I end up making less than minimum wage for all the hours I put in. Even the part-time teaching I sometimes do to supplement my income pays better.

Then on top of it being so hard to get help, veterans faced stereotyping and prejudice. Jimmy had lost a leg defending our country but when somebody murders his wife, everybody immediately assumes it was him. Because after all, vets with PTSD always have anger issues.

By the time I got home, I'd work myself into a full-blown snit.

I marched into the house and headed for the kitchen. Plugging my phone into an outlet to charge, I turned it on. I'd missed a half dozen calls, the most pressing of which were from Max's soon-to-be new owner and from my mother.

I called Pete Sanchez back first and set a time for Wednesday to start his training with Max.

I found the number for Jo Ann Hamilton's office, but I got her voicemail. I left a message explaining who I was and filling her in on what had happened to Jimmy. Maybe she'd at least call and try to cheer him up over the phone.

Then I took a deep breath and called my mother.

I'd say that I have a good relationship with my mom. I can confide in her and I know she'll always have my back. Some people say we're a lot alike. I'm willing to acknowledge that my freckles and ample hips come from her, as does my penchant for saying *crapola.* It's the closest she ever comes to cussing.

I guess I take after her there too–the only semi-naughty word I ever use is *fricking,* as a substitute for the F word. And yeah, okay, my bad temper comes from her side of the family as well.

Overall, she and I get along well, but she's never quite forgiven me for moving almost a thousand miles away from her.

"Hey, kiddo," she answered, her tone light.

"Hey, Mom. Sorry I didn't call back sooner. My phone battery died and I forgot to recharge it."

"You really need to get a landline, sweetheart."

"Can't afford it."

"You could if you'd made that no-good ex of yours pay you alimony."

I held the phone away from my mouth as I blew out air.

"I heard that."

Dang! Aren't old people supposed to become hard of hearing?

Not my mom. She could hear a pin drop twenty yards away.

I debated the value of explaining yet again that the courts these days rarely awarded alimony to an able-bodied female with no minor children.

"You gave up a career to support his. Just taught part-time instead of pursuing your PhD." My mother had read my mind, as usual.

I have a masters degree in counseling psychology. That and a buck-fifty will buy you a cup of coffee at the Mayfair Diner. It didn't qualify me to do much professionally other than teach college part-time, full-time positions being reserved for the folks with doctorates.

I sighed, louder this time and on purpose. The reality was that I hadn't pursued my doctorate because I was sick of going to school, and I hadn't asked for alimony because I wasn't about to tie myself to my jerk of an ex-husband for the rest of my life. Besides the concept of alimony was insulting to a woman in this day and age.

"And being a liberated woman doesn't pay the bills, now does it?" Mom said.

I shook my head at the phone. I so wanted to pace, but I was tied to the wall via the charger's cord.

"How's Ben?" My brother, his wife and their 2.5 rug rats (the youngest still a babe in arms) lived within twenty minutes of our childhood home, which filled my mother with joy and made her harassment of me to move back to Maryland less intense than it probably would otherwise be. I couldn't say I was close to him and his family, but bringing him up was usually a good way to deflect my mother from her critique of my life.

"Benjamin is fine, as is his family." Silence for a moment. "I'm sorry, Marcia. Let's start again. How are you?"

I started to say I was fine, then thought better of it. I wasn't fine at all.

"Not so good, Mom."

Twenty minutes later, I'd poured out the whole story, and my mother had made calming and reassuring noises at all the right moments.

"So what are you going to do?" she asked.

"I think I need to figure out who killed Julie. I need…" What did I need? "This man's been through so much." I heard the tears in my voice and stopped.

A long pause. "Just be careful, sweetheart."

I knew that had cost her. She really wanted to tell me to leave it alone, to not take the risks involved in chasing down a killer.

My throat aching, I said, "I will be. Thanks for listening."

I disconnected and put the phone down on the counter. A cool nose nudged my other hand. I scratched behind Buddy's ears.

Now I was glad my department chair hadn't had a class for me this semester. I would need the time I usually spent grading assignments to conduct an investigation.

I leaned down and touched noses with Buddy. "Hey boy, I hope a psychology degree will help me find a killer."

CHAPTER SEVEN

Having decided to investigate, I was now itching to get started. Over the weekend, I crammed in as much training as I could, so that I could spend most of Monday in Collinsville.

Saturday morning, I did a quick refresher session with Max, to reinforce what he already knew quite well. But there was no such thing as too much training when it came to service dogs.

I had put him inside and had started with Lacy when my cell phone vibrated in my pocket. Since I was practicing the cover command, I figured I could risk taking the phone out and checking it. I stopped and looked at the caller ID, all the while watching Lacy out of the corner of my eye. Sure enough she turned around and faced the way we'd come.

The call was from Becky. "Hey, Beck. Hang on a sec." I started walking again down the length of the yard. Lacy fell into step beside me. I gave her a treat. "Good girl."

"I like to think so," Becky said in my ear.

I laughed. "I'm working with Lacy. What's up?"

"I won't keep you long then. I just wanted to let you know something I found out." Her voice was a bit breathless. "I've got this new client and we were chit-chatting a little, you know, getting comfortable with each other before I started her massage. Long story how we got on the subject of small towns, but it turns out she's from Collinsville."

Lacy was walking sedately beside me. I stopped. She stopped and turned.

"So I said, all casual-like, what a shame it was about the Garretts. Well, she hadn't heard about it, so I told her Julie'd been murdered and Jimmy was accused of killing her."

Wishing Becky would get to the point, I started moving again. Lacy fell into step. I decided to skip the treat. It was time to start making the rewards more intermittent.

Becky's breathless voice continued in my ear. "And she said that she wasn't surprised. 'Did he finally catch on to her affair?' she says."

My own breath caught in my throat. "What? Julie was having an affair?"

"Apparently, or at least that was the rumor around town, although nobody seemed to know who the guy was."

I'd stopped moving, but Lacy was doing her got-your-back routine just fine.

"It was while Jimmy was overseas on his last deployment," Becky said.

"Wait. They weren't living in Collinsville then." This time when I started moving again, I gave Lacy a treat.

"Seems that Julie moved back there while Jimmy was overseas. She was living with her grandmother. The rumor was, when grandma went to her canasta club meetings, Julie had a visitor."

"Hmm, I'm going down there Monday to see Jimmy. I was going to poke around some. This gives me a thread to start pulling on."

Chatty Becky suddenly fell silent.

"Don't worry," I said. "I'll be careful."

"You shouldn't be doing that alone."

"You volunteering to go with me?" I asked.

"Wish I could, but I've got clients all day."

I stopped moving. Lacy shifted into position facing behind me. "I'll have Buddy with me."

The big boy was lying under the magnolia tree at the end of the yard. He lifted his chin off his paws at the sound of his name. I shook my head at him.

I took two steps and turned to head back toward the house. Lacy fell into step. I stopped. She pivoted around again, facing the way we'd come.

"Well, I'll let you get back to your training," Becky said.

"I never stopped. Lacy is doing exactly what she's supposed to be doing." I started moving and the dog fell into step and looked up at me. I swear she was smiling. "Gotta go. Thanks for the info."

"Happy to help. Hey, be careful, okay?" Usually Becky's voice had this little lilt to it, as if she were on the verge of laughing at any moment. But now she sounded so solemn, it made my chest ache.

"I will be. And Beck…"

"What?"

"I love you, too."

I disconnected and pocketed my phone. Then I stopped just short of the deck. Lacy immediately took up her position facing behind me.

I stepped up on the deck and she hopped up next to me. I gave her a vigorous ear scratch. "You're such a smart dog!" She grinned at me.

I took a figurative step back, reminding myself not to get too attached to this sweet dog. "Your new owner is going to love you to pieces."

You have to love dogs to do what I do, spending all day most days in their company, following a rigorous training schedule. But that love of the animals also makes it hard, when it comes time to give them up to their rightful owners.

I'm not sure how I would describe Jimmy's mood on Monday morning. Despondent would have required more energy than he seemed to possess.

Once we were back in the cell area, I released Buddy's leash and signaled he was off duty. He raced around the corner and jammed his nose between the bars of Jimmy's cell, his back end wiggling so hard I feared he might dislocate something.

"Hi, boy." Jimmy's voice, low and monotone.

As I rounded the corner, Jimmy was slowly pushing himself up from his cot. He hobbled across the cell.

"What's the matter?" I pointed to his leg.

He shrugged. "It's hard to get the stump clean, standing up in the shower." He paused as if he had to regain his strength before continuing. "And I only get to shower every other day." He shrugged again. "'Course, it's not like I'm working up a sweat in here."

Buddy nudged his hand with his nose. Jimmy gave him a half-hearted pat on the head.

"Would you like some books or something?" I asked.

He shook his head. "I'm not much of a reader."

"Have you heard anything new from your lawyer?"

He silently shook his head again.

My mind cast around for something else to say. It's hard to hold a conversation with a depressed person. "Why did you and Julie move here? I mean I get the wanting to be close to family, but was that the only reason?"

Buddy licked Jimmy's fingers and whined softly. Jimmy gave him another pat.

"Actually, the fact her brother runs the bank was a drawback to movin' here. But Julie owns…" He pressed his lips together and closed his eyes. Then he opened them again. They were shiny with unshed tears. "Julie *owned* the house. Her grandma left it to her. And she left Julie half of her interest in the bank, so her brother had to let her work there."

"Oh." Shame on me–I'd assumed Julie was a teller or something. "So she and her brother didn't get along so well."

Jimmy sighed. "Yes and no. They didn't much as kids. Julie said he called her the little interloper. I guess he'd gotten used to being an only child before she was born."

"There was a big age difference between them?"

"Yeah. Eleven years. But they got along okay as adults. We spent a couple of Christmases at John's house. Heck, I even got the big brother speech from him when we got married, about how I'd better take good care of his baby sister or…" His voice choked. He stopped and sucked in air, leaning against the bars as if it were too much effort to stand upright.

I had a flash of doubt. Had he really killed his wife in a fit of rage? Or was his upset just grief?

He shook his head, then looked me in the eye. "Julie lived with her grandma when I was overseas. She said they got on okay then."

Buddy whimpered and sniffed at the edge of a tray that rested just inside the cell on the floor. He looked up at me, asking permission to nab one of the strips of greasy bacon resting next to congealed eggs on Jimmy's breakfast plate. It didn't look like the man had eaten more than a few bites.

I opened my mouth to admonish Jimmy that he needed to eat, then caught myself. I wasn't sure he'd appreciate me playing the mother role. I opted for a gentler comment instead. "It looks like you don't have much appetite."

He grimaced. "Hard to get enthusiastic about eatin' when Doris is my waitress. That woman could curdle milk just by lookin' at it."

Buddy gazed up at me again, hope in his eyes. My throat tightened at the realization that already the dog was looking to me for permission, not Jimmy. But the man hadn't seemed to notice.

"Can Buddy have some of your bacon?"

"Sure. Okay, boy," he said to the dog.

Buddy dropped down onto his tummy and poked his nose into the cell to catch the end of the strip of bacon between his teeth. It was gone in one gulp. He looked up at Jimmy.

"It's okay. Take them all, boy."

Buddy scarfed them down, then stood and licked Jimmy's fingers again, a canine thank you.

But the conversation between the humans had stalled completely.

Suddenly I had an idea. "Hey, can you hold onto Buddy for a

few minutes." I clipped the leash back onto the dog's collar and handed the other end of it through the bars. I shuffled my feet a little, implying that I needed to use the restroom.

Jimmy winced and shifted his weight off of his prosthesis. "Sure."

"I won't be long." I hoped that was true. It was obviously uncomfortable for Jimmy to stand.

I'd told a nonverbal fib. After the long drive, the restroom had been my first stop once inside the police station. But I wanted to talk to the sheriff, and I preferred to avoid a verbal tussle with Doris over whether or not I could do that. Without Buddy in tow, there was a good chance I could slip around behind her and get to the sheriff's office door before she could stop me.

It worked. I knocked softly on the half-open door.

"Come in."

"Hey," Doris yelled. "You can't just barge–"

I slipped through the door and pushed it closed behind me, cutting off the woman's protests.

The sheriff gave me a big smile, his blue eyes dancing. "Hey, Ms. Banks. How are you today?"

I noticed there was a little cleft in the middle of his chin, which added to the rugged look. I tried not to stare. "I'm good. How are you?"

"I'm fine. What can I do for you?" He gestured toward an empty chair in front of his desk.

I walked over and perched on the edge of it.

"Where's the dog?" the sheriff asked conversationally.

"Uh, I hope you don't mind, but I left him back with Jimmy for a few minutes."

The sheriff cocked his head to one side. "Guess there's no harm in that."

"I was actually hoping you would let me leave Buddy with him for an hour or two. I think it would cheer Jimmy up. And I've got some errands to run." I waved a hand in the general direction of Lakeland, implying I would be heading over to that metropolis to do some shopping.

The sheriff's friendly expression sobered. "That's not exactly standard operating procedure."

"I realize that, but Jimmy seems pretty depressed. What harm can it do?"

"What if we need to take Jimmy out of his cell for something? Will the dog come after us?"

"Probably not. He's not an attack dog. The day Julie died, he was protecting Jimmy because he was down on the ground, and he was protecting his home, his territory."

"What if Jimmy tells him to attack, to try to escape?"

"Buddy wouldn't know what to do with that command. And honestly, I don't think Jimmy has the energy to try to escape. Where would he go?"

"Okay, we'll put the dog in with him while you're gone." The sheriff started to push himself to a stand.

"Uh, there's something else…"

He sank back into his chair.

"Jimmy needs a shower chair, and he needs to be able to shower daily. His stump is getting irritated because he can't clean it properly while trying to balance on one leg."

"Don't know where I'd come up with a shower chair."

I bristled but tried to hide my irritation. "You're required to accommodate his needs."

The sheriff's jaw tightened. "Yeah, but I can't exactly pull a shower chair out of my bu…uh, desk drawer, now can I?"

"Haven't you ever heard of the ADA?"

"The assistant district attorney?" I almost missed the slight quirk of the corners of his lips. He was messing with me.

I might have found his feigned confusion amusing if I wasn't so annoyed. "Nooo." I dragged the word out. "The Americans with Disabilities Act. It's–"

He raised his hand in the air, palm out. "No need to get huffy. I'm not trying to avoid doing what's right, with or without a law that says I have to. I just don't know where I'll get a shower chair on short notice."

I ducked my head to hide the heat rising in my cheeks.

Just because I've got red highlights in my hair doesn't mean I have to act like a redhead. My inner voice sounded surprisingly like my mother's. Why was I so quick to heat up with this guy?

Uh, duh! You're attracted to him.

That wasn't what I meant by heated up, I replied internally. I could have sworn I heard a faint snicker.

Out loud, I said, "The hardware store may have one."

The sheriff let out an exaggerated sigh. "You're gonna make me deal with old man Kroger?"

I looked up and made eye contact. He was grinning at me.

My insides relaxed and I gave him a small smile back. "Afraid so."

"Could I get your cell phone number? If he doesn't have one, I could call you and maybe you could look for one down in Lakeland?"

My cheeks heated up again, this time because I'd been tripped up by my own fib about going to Lakeland. "Uh, sure." I fumbled around in my purse and found one of my business cards, a little tattered around the edges.

My GPS readily found Jimmy's street again. It was an older neighborhood, not much different than most of the small side streets in Mayfair. The houses were well kept, each nestled on a generous lot thick with palm trees and live oaks and tall azaleas about to burst into full bloom. Their cement block or clapboard walls were mostly painted white or beige, with an occasional pale green or yellow adding some variety. Roofs of light-colored shingles or metal reflected away the Florida sun in a shimmering haze.

I pulled up in front of the Garretts' house. I know it's only a building, but with the blinds pulled down on a bright sunny day, it looked sad.

Theirs was a corner lot, a bit bigger than the others, but the house was no larger than its neighbors. Not all that imposing for a couple–Julie's grandparents, that is–who'd founded the town and owned the bank. My guess was they'd never upgraded their living quarters to reflect their success. With only one child, Julie's and John's father, perhaps they'd figured the house satisfied their needs so why go more upscale. Or perhaps they'd feared the townspeople would see it as uppity if they'd built a big, fancy house.

I wasn't sure whether Miss Shirley, the gossipy neighbor, lived to the right of the Garretts or behind them. I mentally flipped a coin. It came up heads for the right side.

When an elderly woman answered the door, I figured it was an omen that this was going to be a good day. "Are you Miss Shirley?"

She squinted through a ratty screen door at me. "Who wants to know?"

"My name is Marcia Banks. I'm…" Dang, I should've given some thought to how to present myself. "I'm a friend of the Garretts."

"Ain't never seen you around town."

"No, ma'am. I knew them before they moved here."

"Julie's lived here most all her life."

"Yes, ma'am, but I knew them when they were living in that house down near Lakeland."

The woman made a scoffing noise in the back of her throat. "She shoulda stayed here with her grandma, 'stead of marryin' that Army boy."

"Jimmy's a former Marine." The words were out of my mouth before I'd thought them through. I was trying to get on this woman's good side, that is, if she had one. Probably not the best thing to argue with her.

"Marine, Navy, Army. What difference does it make?"

It made a lot of difference to any member of one of those branches of the armed services, but I pressed my teeth together.

"I'd really like to ask you a few questions, ma'am." I tried to pump some sadness into my voice. "I just can't believe Julie's gone. And I find it even harder to believe that Jimmy killed her. They seemed so happy together."

The old woman made the scoffing sound again, stepped closer to the screen door and leaned her head back. I realized she was examining my face through the bottom part of her bifocals.

"Guess ya might as well come on in." She turned and headed into the dark coolness of her house.

I opened the screen door, the hinges screeching softly, and followed her.

Miss Shirley wasn't so bad once I got her talking. I tried not to wince every time I took a sip of the sweet tea she'd pressed on me. I'd figured it wouldn't have helped my cause to ask for unsweetened.

I was making what I hoped were pleasant-sounding "I'm listening" noises and trying to figure out how to bring up Julie's alleged affair, when the woman went there on her own.

"'Course I'm not the least bit surprised those two finally had a blow up, what with the foolin' around that girl did when he was overseas."

"Fooling around?" I tried to look surprised. "Julie was having an affair?"

Miss Shirley nodded, a grave expression on her face. But I had a hunch she was enjoying having a new audience for her gossip.

"Like clockwork, every Wednesday mornin'. Victoria'd go off to play canasta with her friends and I'd hear rustlin' in their backyard just a few minutes later."

Hoping my face was exhibiting the appropriate level of shock, I said, "Do you know who it was?"

"No. The bushes is too thick on Victoria's side."

Obviously bushes on Miss Shirley's side would have long since been sacrificed to the gossip gods.

"I only caught a flash of movement now and then, of someone goin' up on the back porch. Then Julie'd let them in. And an hour or so later, they'd leave again, long before Victoria got home."

"You didn't see anything that would identify him?"

"Nope, except when I did see movement, well it looked like the man was wearing somethin' tan. But that don't mean much 'round here. Lots of men wear tan work clothes. Why, Andy Kroger has trouble keepin' them in stock over at the hardware store."

"He sells clothes there?"

"Just work clothes and camouflage for huntin' and such. Nearest department store's in Polk City."

"Julie didn't have to work on Wednesdays?" I asked.

Miss Shirley's hand, holding her iced tea glass, stopped half-way to her mouth. She narrowed her eyes slightly. But then her desire for a fresh audience must have overcome her suspicions regarding why I knew so little about my so-called friends. "She wasn't workin' at the bank then. Her folks died before her grand-dad, in a car accident out on I-75. He left the bank to his wife and his grandkids, one third each, plus a fair amount of money. But Julie wouldn't have gotten control over her money 'til she turned thirty, which would've been next year. It was in one of those, what do ya call 'em?"

"A trust fund?"

"Yeah, a trust fund. As for the bank, John–that's her brother–he wouldn't let her get involved with how things was run there, said Julie was too young and inexperienced. Victoria didn't want to make waves so she let him have his way."

Then Miss Shirley grinned.

A shiver ran down my spine. It was not a nice grin.

"John got his comeuppance when Victoria passed. She left half her stocks to each of them, so'd they'd own the bank, half and half, even-steven. He couldn't keep Julie out after that."

"You don't like John Collins?"

Miss Shirley gave me a startled look. "I ain't got nothin' against the boy."

Oh, so you like to see anyone get their comeuppance.

I kept that thought to myself as I politely thanked her for the iced tea and headed for the door.

As I was about to step through it, I realized I'd forgotten something. I turned back toward the elderly woman. "Uh, could I ask another question?"

Miss Shirley nodded.

"Were you the anonymous caller who tipped off the sheriff's department about the Garretts' door sitting open?"

She shook her head.

"Do you have any idea who it might have been?"

"No."

I thanked her again and made my escape, I mean exit.

CHAPTER EIGHT

Having survived Miss Shirley, I figured I could probably handle Jimmy's sister-in-law, but I didn't know where she lived. A quick Google search on my phone resulted in way too many hits for John Collins. Narrowing the search by adding Collinsville, Florida only produced a couple of articles about the bank.

Leaving my car parked where it was, I walked back toward Main Street and the diner.

The little restaurant was busy, with a couple of waitresses scooting back and forth from the kitchen to the tables full of hungry customers. Jane stood in the middle of the chaos, ignoring her overworked staff. She was next to a table of men wolfing down their lunches, her hand resting casually on the back of one of the booth's benches.

She turned slightly, saw me near the door, and gave me the evil eye.

I pretended she had smiled at me sweetly.

"Afternoon, ma'am." Jane wasn't much older than I was, but I figured a bit of deference might gain me some ground. "I don't suppose you have a local phone book, do you?"

She jerked her head toward the back of the restaurant without saying anything.

"Thank you." I gave her my best fake smile, the one I had honed while married to Ted when I'd had to attend various orchestra-related social events. Then I made my way past the overflowing tables and booths. My stomach rumbled in response to the enticing fragrances emanating from the diner's kitchen, but Jane's scowling face dampened my appetite. I'd grab some lunch later, on the way back home.

As I passed the booth next to where she stood, she leaned over and whispered something in a man's ear. He looked my way and grinned. It was the kind of grin the school bully has on his face as he approaches you.

The man was Deputy Frank. My fake smile faltered some.

For the briefest moment, Jane's hand rested on Frank's shoulder as she smirked at me.

I kept moving.

In the back of the diner near the restrooms, I was astounded to find a real honest to goodness pay phone, with a phone book tethered to it. I fumbled in my purse for a pen and jotted down the address listed for John Collins, Jr. on a grocery receipt. The book looked kind of old. I hoped this was the current John Collins and not his deceased father.

As I was leaving the diner, Deputy Frank was paying his check at the cash register near the front. He'd seemed nice enough the other day at the sheriff's department, but today he was giving off different vibes.

Or maybe it was Jane's attitude and the overall atmosphere of the diner that had me on edge. I maneuvered past the deputy without making eye contact and pushed open the door.

"See ya later, Frank." Jane's voice from behind me, downright simpering.

Resisting the urge to make gagging noises, I got the heck out of there.

Sheila Collins was not what I'd expected. I'd imagined a well-groomed banker's wife with a servant or two to handle mundane things such as answering doorbells and changing diapers. Instead a slightly overweight, fortyish woman in navy sweats answered the door of the sprawling, modern rancher (apparently John, Jr. had no qualms about flaunting his success).

Wisps of the woman's mousy brown hair escaped from a ponytail secured on the back of her head with a scrunchie. The toddler on her hip was sucking her thumb and staring at me with wide eyes.

Wondering if this was a babysitter, I said, "Mrs. Collins?"

She shaded her eyes with her free hand and squinted at me as I stood on her sunny porch. "Yes."

"Uh, I'm Marcia Banks, a friend of Julie and Jimmy. I just wanted to stop by and offer my condolences. Is this Ida Mae? My, how she's grown." I'd never laid eyes on the child, but how would this woman know that.

Mrs. Collins continued to stare at me for another beat. "You want to come in?"

"If you don't mind. I can't stay long, though."

She switched the silent toddler to her other hip and led the way down a short entrance hallway to a spacious living room. Skylights and a sliding glass door made it light and airy-looking. But the impression of affluence created by leather furniture in rich earth tones and a plush white carpet was marred by toys scattered everywhere.

Mrs. Collins gestured toward one of two tan sofas. It was longer than my entire living room.

"You want to take her? I need to clean this mess up." She gestured vaguely at the scattered toys.

"Uh, she probably won't remember me. It's been awhile." Truth was kids made me nervous, and the younger they were, the more likely they were to give me hives.

Sheila Collins shrugged and lowered the toddler into a mesh contraption in a corner.

I settled onto the sofa, surreptitiously stroking the buttery-soft leather.

Mrs. Collins picked toys up off the floor and tossed them into a plastic crate in another corner. "I don't know what's going to happen if Jimmy's convicted. Our kids are mostly grown. Our son's in college. We're really not equipped to raise another child."

"There isn't any other family, is there?"

"'Fraid not."

Ida Mae had grabbed one of her toys, a small square of cloth with a stuffed monkey's head attached to one corner. She was sucking on its ear. I felt for the tyke but that made me no more inclined to try to interact with her.

Sheila scooped up the last of the toys from the floor, a small plastic doll wearing nothing but a diaper. "Where are my manners? Can I get you some coffee or sweet tea?"

"No, no thank you. I'm fine." I was searching for a way to direct the conversation toward who might have killed Julie. "So I guess you'd rather Jimmy turn out to be not guilty."

Okay, that was lame.

Mrs. Collins shrugged and perched on the other end of the sofa.

I tried again. "Did they fight a lot? I always thought they got along well."

Another shrug. "I thought so too. I never saw them fight. Julie was pretty easygoing, and Jimmy seemed devoted to her. Of course I haven't seen much of them since John's grandmother died last year." She dropped her gaze to her lap and fidgeted with the doll she still held.

"Really? But that's when they moved back here, wasn't it?"

"Yeah, but my husband… he, uh, wasn't thrilled with his grandmother's will. Since he'd been running the bank for almost a decade, he thought he would get controlling interest." She looked nervously around the room. "But I shouldn't be boring you with all that family stuff. John says I blabber too much."

I glanced at a grouping of family photos on the nearest wall. Assuming the grinning young man in several of them was their son, I said, "So you said your boy's in college. What's he studying?"

Mrs. Collins visibly relaxed. She smiled for the first time since she'd opened the front door. "He wants to be a doctor, and he's got the grades to make it happen." She dropped her gaze again.

"John wants him to come into the bank though."

I gestured toward one of the photos, a teenager in a cheerleading outfit. "Is that your daughter, Mrs. Collins?"

She nodded. "Please, call me Sheila. Mrs. Collins was John's grandmother."

"And I'm Marcia. What's your daughter interested in doing?"

The woman's face pinched together in a pained look. "She's the one with a head for numbers. I mean Johnny's good enough with math to handle the science required to be pre-med. But Sally's the true mathematician."

"So is she likely to follow in her dad's footsteps?"

Sheila Collins gave a slight shake of her head. "Maybe," came out of her mouth.

I didn't need a PhD in psychology to realize that all was not well in this household. Indeed, Mrs. Collins had that nervous, defeated look I'd seen before, on the face of one of my acquaintances from the symphony circles in Maryland. There'd been a bit of a scandal when she'd finally gotten up the nerve to leave her bass-playing husband. It had come out during their messy divorce that he'd been beating her for years.

I wasn't going to assume John Collins was a wife-batterer, but he certainly seemed to be a bit domineering. And apparently a believer in the old assumption that certain jobs were done by men, not women. Sons followed in their father's footsteps, not daughters.

I couldn't think of a way to bring up the affair Julie was allegedly having so I decided to be more straightforward. I leaned toward Mrs. Collins. "Did Julie have any enemies?"

She seemed startled by the question. "No, of course not." More fidgeting with the plastic doll in her lap. "As I said, she was very easygoing."

"How about her friends? Who had she gotten close to in town?" Maybe that would bring us around to who she might be having an affair with.

"Mainly Doris. They were friends from way back."

"Isn't Doris a good bit older than Julie?"

Sheila Collins shook her head, then nodded, as if she wasn't sure how to answer what I'd thought was a pretty concrete question. Age is age.

"Doris isn't as old as she looks. She hasn't weathered well."

I suppressed the urge to smile. That was a great way to describe Doris's weathered skin and raspy voice. "How old is she?"

Sheila Collins gave me a sidelong, censoring glance. Apparently she considered it impolite to directly inquire about a woman's age, even if the woman wasn't present. "She and I were in school together. She's thirty-eight."

I suspect I failed to hide my shock. Neither of these women had aged well. And if Sheila Collins was the same age, she'd had her son when she was barely out of high school.

"So you're a few years younger than your husband?" I was fishing for her exact age, not that it mattered all that much.

Mrs. Collins blushed. "Yes. He's forty." Her eyes softened as they focused on the photos on the wall. "We met in high school. He was quarterback of the football team." She paused, still staring at the photos. "Would you believe I was his homecoming queen? And I was just a sophomore."

Glancing at her daughter in her cheerleader get-up, yes, I could believe that.

"We were the classic high school sweethearts," she said wistfully.

I was tempted to ask her if she'd ever really loved him, but that would be way too rude. And I already suspected what the answer would be. She wouldn't be the first nor the last young woman to fall in love with the idea of being in love. And who was I to throw stones, after the debacle of my marriage.

I'd probably gotten all I was going to out of her, but then I decided to give it one more try, to be sure I was being thorough. "So you can't imagine anyone who'd want to hurt Julie? I'd really like to see Jimmy out of that jail and taking care of his little girl again." I waved a hand in the direction of the mesh thingie, in which Ida Mae was now lying down, her eyelids at half-mast.

Sheila shook her head, her mouth turned down in a sad frown. "No. I'm afraid it's gotta be him. But I'm sure it was an accident. He just lost his temper."

I'll bet you make similar excuses for your husband. A thought I kept to myself.

I rose from the sofa. "Well, I'd better be getting along. It's a long drive home."

Sheila rose to show me to the door.

I paused by the mesh thingie and blew a kiss in Ida Mae's direction. "I don't want to wake her up," I whispered, in case Sheila was wondering why I hadn't shown more affection toward the child.

Once outside, I headed back toward the sheriff's department.

I really wanted to talk to Julie's brother too. Well actually, I didn't. The thought of that conversation made my stomach roil. But talk to him I must. And also to Doris. Another conversation I was dreading.

Today, however, I was out of time. I needed to get back to Max and Lacy.

The sheriff wasn't in when I arrived to collect Buddy. I let out the breath I'd been holding. I wasn't going to get caught in the Lakeland errand-running fib.

I'd gotten myself and the dog as far as my car and had beeped open the door locks, when someone called my name. "Ms. Banks."

I looked up.

Crapola.

Sheriff Haines was headed my way.

Buddy did his job and inserted himself between me and the approaching person, but his tail was wagging slightly.

Hmm, so his dislike of Doris and Deputy Frank isn't about the uniform.

Speaking of which, the sheriff filled his out nicely, his broad shoulders and chest putting a slight strain on the khaki fabric. As usual, he had his shirt sleeves rolled up, exposing tanned, muscular arms.

I noted a funny little quivering in my core.

Don't go there! a voice in my head said.

A girl can look, I answered it.

"Ms. Banks, I'm glad I caught up with you." He took off his hat and wiped the sweat off his forehead with the back of his hand.

"You didn't call, so I assume you found a shower chair."

The sheriff grinned. "Yeah, Kroger's had one, but it needed a shower of its own before I could give it to Jimmy to use."

Ignoring the warmth in my cheeks–which of course was due to the warm sun, *not* the proximity of the sheriff's fine masculine physique–I returned the man's smile. "What can I do for you, Sheriff?"

His blue eyes clouded over. "I hear you're asking questions around town."

Wow, small town gossip usually spreads quickly but this place was lightning fast. I squinted up at the sheriff's face. "No law against that, is there?"

"Not as long as you don't interfere with an ongoing investigation."

"I don't see the *ongoing* part happening." The words slipped out before I could stop them, the tone sharper than was probably wise. This guy might have the authority to toss me out of town. He could certainly keep me from seeing Jimmy again.

He blew out air. "Look, I'm not going to let Jimmy be railroaded here, if he didn't do it."

Hmm, that sounded like the sheriff was starting to believe Jimmy's protests of innocence.

I should have made nice-nice. After all, the man had located a shower chair and was giving Jimmy the benefit of the doubt. But some perverse part of me had taken over. I frowned up at him. "The best thing you could do for Jimmy right now is get someone else to serve him his meals. That Doris doesn't like him and he's getting more and more depressed, thinking everybody's against him." I hadn't planned to say any of that. It just kind of tumbled out.

The sheriff gave me a long, hard look. "I haven't got anyone else. I can't spare one of my men to hang around the office."

Okay, that ticked me off. "Oh, so only women can do office duty?"

He blew out air again. His mouth moved as if he were mumbling to himself–counting to ten maybe. "Doris is not a trained officer. I let her wear a uniform because it makes her feel good and when people come in, they're less likely to give her grief."

Way to go, Banks.

"Oh, sorry," I said out loud.

"Look, stop poking around, okay?" The sheriff offered up a smile, which was quite gracious of him, all things considered. "I don't want anything happening to my favorite redhead."

"I'm not a redhead. I'm a brunette." *Why* was I arguing with him? I loved it that the Florida sun had found some red pigment in my hair and had decided to highlight it.

He reached out and fingered a wisp that had come loose from my ponytail. My hair follicles tingled.

"Looks red enough to me," he said in a gentle voice. Then he hooked the hair behind my ear. "Seriously, investigating a murder is dangerous. You need to keep that cute, freckled nose out of it."

I would have been insulted by the familiarity of "my favorite redhead" and the condescension implied in the "cute, freckled nose" comment, if I hadn't been so busy dealing with my body's reaction to his fleeting touch of my ear. A jolt of something had shot through me.

If we were up in the cold, dry north, I could have blamed it on static electricity. But down here in humid, warm Florida, I had no such lie I could tell myself.

It was just plain old electricity.

Crapola!

CHAPTER NINE

The next morning, I crammed in an intensive training session with Lacy and a refresher one with Max so that I could return to Collinsville that afternoon. I'd called on the way home the day before and scheduled an appointment with John Collins at the bank, using my married name. I'd told the young woman who'd answered the phone that I was thinking about moving to the town and wanted to find out what services their bank provided.

After a quick, early lunch, I dressed in the one custom-tailored suit I still owned, back from my days of hobnobbing with the symphony crowd. Then I tamed my hair into a French braid, tucking the ends up underneath to make a sleek bun.

Buddy stayed home this time. I wanted to fly under the sheriff's radar if possible.

With only minor breaches of the speed limit, I arrived a few minutes early for my two o'clock appointment.

I must have looked the part of a well-to-do potential customer. John Collins' eyes lit up when he came out of his office and spotted me, waiting with legs demurely crossed on a leather couch nearby. He walked toward me, beaming, his hand extended. "How do you do, Ms. Goldman?"

A young woman, sitting at a desk across from the small waiting area, shot me a hard look.

I stood and smoothed down the raw silk skirt of my suit. "I'm well, thank you, Mr. Collins. How are you?" Hey, I know how to be formal when the occasion calls for it.

"I'm good." More flashing of white teeth. "Welcome to our little town." He ushered me into his office and gestured toward a sitting area at one end of the spacious room.

I settled into an antique wingback chair. "I haven't quite decided yet if I'm going to relocate here. But the climate is certainly conducive."

He smiled at me from his chair on the other side of an oversized coffee table. When I didn't elaborate, he asked, "Conducive to what?"

I gave him a mock startled look. "Why, raising horses. You've never heard of the Goldman stables?" Mind you, I didn't say I owned the Goldman stables, which I'd never heard of either. The morals my parents had instilled in me didn't allow for flat-out lying, but I wasn't above implication, innuendo, and a small fib here and there, for a good cause.

He looked appropriately chagrined. "No, I'm afraid I haven't. This is definitely horse country though. Lots of fine farms around here."

"Yes, that reminds me. Could you give me the name of a good real estate agent in the area?"

"Certainly."

I raised a finger in the air in what I hoped was an imperious manner. Then I lifted my Gucci knock-off from the floor and extracted a small bound address book and a gold pen. The latter had been a present from Ted on our second and last anniversary. (Who gives his wife a *pen* for their anniversary? Sheez!)

John Collins gave me a name and phone number and I made a show of jotting them down.

I planned to pass the referral along to Jimmy after he got out of jail. I doubted he'd want to keep their house.

"What would you like to know about our humble establishment, Ms. Goldman?"

I smiled graciously. "Please call me Marsha, Mr. Collins. Everybody does."

It was the truth. Everybody did mispronounce my name when

they first met me.

Another beaming smile from Collins. "And I'm John. How can I help you, Marsha?"

"I wanted to make sure your bank can handle substantial short-term loans. Sometimes a good buy comes along for a prize brood mare, just when the stable is cash-poor."

He looked a smidgen worried. "How much is substantial?"

"Usually between thirty and fifty thousand." I'd done some quick research the night before on top-of-the-line brood mares in the breeds that were usually used for horse racing.

"That shouldn't be a problem, assuming your credit is good," Collins said. "But honestly it would save you money to use your personal assets at times like that."

I frowned at him. "There are no blemishes on my credit, John." This was true because I had *no* credit. My half of the proceeds from the sale of the marital abode in Maryland had provided enough cash to buy my little house down here outright. And although my silver sedan was a step up from the rattletrap van I'd brought down with me, it was still a secondhand, older model, also bought with cash.

Collins tried to regain my favor with a big smile. "Of course I assumed that. It's not really in my best interests to say so, but you'd save a lot on interest if you covered such expenditures from personal funds."

I got it, a little late on the uptake, that he was fishing for how much I was worth personally.

"The stables are a separate legal entity." Surely there was a Goldman Stables somewhere in the U.S., and it was most definitely a separate entity from me. "It's cleaner if I don't mingle resources."

"Of course. You would be transferring your personal banking to us though, wouldn't you?"

"Oh, certainly. That goes without saying, if I do decide to move to the area."

"Excellent. Would you like a tour of our vault?" He started

to push up out of his chair.

I raised the imperious finger again. “In a moment. First, I have some questions about the town. I want to make sure it’s the kind of community I will feel comfortable in.” I leaned slightly forward in my chair. “I heard there was a murder here recently.”

“Oh, well yes. But it was the result of a domestic dispute. We certainly don’t have any cold-blooded killers hanging around town.” He gave a hearty chuckle that sounded totally fake.

“Wait. The young woman who was killed, wasn’t her maiden name Collins? Was she a relative?”

His sad expression was only slightly more genuine than the chuckle. “Afraid so. My sister actually.”

My hand flew to my mouth. “Oh my. How rude of me, and unfeeling. I wouldn’t have brought it up if I’d realized. Were you two close?”

“Not particularly. Julie was hard to get along with.”

Humph. That’s not what the rest of the town says.

“Still, what a shock for you and your family. My condolences. You say it was a domestic dispute. Her boyfriend?”

“Thank you, and no, it was her husband. He’s an ex-Marine, has anger issues.”

I was prepared for the prejudicial comment so it wasn’t hard to hide my anger. “So they’re sure he did it?”

Collins snorted. “He was found passed out drunk at nine in the morning, one room over from her body.”

“That doesn’t necessarily mean he killed her.” I produced a mock shudder. “I’m afraid you haven’t convinced me that there isn’t a killer running around loose.”

“The bedroom was a shambles. It looked like they’d had a fight, and Julie…” He dropped his gaze to the coffee table. “Her head was bashed in.”

I grimaced. “Maybe she interrupted a burglary, and then her husband walked in after the burglar had killed her.”

Collins took a deep breath and blew it out. “I’m not going to say that isn’t a possibility, but we’ve never had a burglary in this town for as long as I can remember. And I've lived here all my life."

I arched my eyebrows at him. "Never?"

"Never. Oh, we've had kids shoplift sometimes, but most people don't even lock their houses. This is a very safe town, Ms. Goldman."

"Marsha." I gave him a small smile. "Well, thank you for easing my worries, especially since it's a painful subject for you."

"No problem. Would you like that tour of the vault now?"

"No thank you. I'm sure it's quite secure." I was disappointed that I hadn't learned more from Collins, but I couldn't think of any more questions that wouldn't sound strange coming from a potential bank customer. I picked up my purse and rose from my chair. "I'm staying with friends in Orlando and we're due at another friend's house for cocktails at five. I must be getting back."

"Oh, who are you visiting? I know a lot of folks in Orlando's social circles."

I felt my eyes go wide before I could catch myself. That's what I got for ad-libbing. I tried to turn the fearful look into one of surprise. "Why the O'Connors, Clay and Marilyn. Do you know them?"

He shook his head. "No, those names don't ring a bell."

No wonder, since I'd only that moment made them up.

I gave him my most charming smile. "It's a big city. Thank you for your time, John. I'll be in touch."

I prayed my knees didn't look as wobbly as they felt as I walked out of his office. The young woman at the desk near his door gave me another hard look. I made an educated guess that she was his administrative assistant. I felt her eyes burning into my back as I moved across the marble expanse of the bank's floor.

I'd parked a block away, in case John Collins knew what kind of car Marcia Banks, versus Marsha Goldman, drove. I waited until I was safely locked inside it before I let out my breath.

As I drove to the sheriff's office, I tried to figure out how to approach Doris. We hadn't exactly gotten off on a good footing.

Indeed, she would no doubt stomp on my foot if given half a chance, or any other body part that came within striking distance.

I didn't particularly want to run into the sheriff either, if I could help it. He would definitely wonder why I was dressed to the nines and might conclude I was still "poking my nose" into his investigation.

At the sheriff's department, I drove around behind the building. By its back exit, I saw what I'd suspected would be there–cigarette stubs scattered on the gravel. Parking half a block down in the alley, I watched that back door.

About fifteen minutes later, Doris came through it. I smirked a little to myself.

She pulled a pack of cigarettes out of her shirt pocket and lit up. I jumped out of my car and walked briskly toward her.

She tilted her head to one side. "Oh, it's you. Didn't recognize you at first in that get-up." Closing her eyes, she took a long drag, then blew out smoke. "Where's the mutt?"

"I couldn't bring him today. I had some business in Lakeland." Okay, that was a flat-out lie, but I had to give some excuse for being there *sans* Buddy and wearing raw silk.

Doris shrugged.

I knew I only had the few minutes it would take for her to get her nicotine hit so I plunged right in. "Look, I know you think Jimmy killed Julie, but I don't think he did. You were her friend. Maybe you can help me figure out who really hurt her."

She squinted at me through a veil of smoke from the cigarette dangling from her lips. When she didn't tell me to get lost, I forged ahead. "I've heard that she might have had an affair when she was living here before, while Jimmy was overseas. Do you know anything about that?"

Doris took the cigarette out of her mouth. "Maybe."

"Do you know who the guy was?"

She studied me for another second, then shook her head. "She never said. She didn't want to be disloyal to Jimmy, but she was lonely."

"Do you have any suspicions about who it was? Maybe they had gotten back together and something happened and they fought."

Doris shook her head again. "I got the impression it was definitely over." Her gaze flicked away from mine. "She only wanted Jimmy once he was home again."

"Any hint of who it was?" I asked again.

She stared at the ground, using the toe of her brown oxford to stir around a couple of old butts.

"You cared about her, didn't you?" I said. "You want her killer brought to justice, right? If it's Jimmy, so be it. But if it's not and he's convicted, her killer will get away scot-free."

She looked up at me, her eyes red-rimmed. "I don't know who it was, and I think you're barkin' up the wrong tree."

"So what's the right tree?"

She shrugged. "Julie'd been preoccupied lately. She had something on her mind."

"What?"

Doris glanced over her shoulder, I guess to make sure we were still alone. But then she said, "I don't know. She wouldn't tell me. At first she said nothin' was wrong when I asked what was botherin' her. A few days before she died, she went all quiet again, and I pushed her some. She said she weren't ready to talk about it. Had to check some things out first."

"Something at the bank?"

"Don't know."

I was wracking my brain for more questions. Doris dropped her cigarette on the ground and stepped on it. I was out of time.

"What can you tell me about her brother?" I asked, more to keep her engaged than anything else.

With a slight sneer on her face, Doris said, "He likes to act all high and mighty, got his so-called friends amongst the rich folks in Lakeland and Orlando. But underneath all that, he's just a good ole Florida boy."

"You don't like him?"

"Never said that."

"Anything else you can tell me that might be useful?"

"Yeah. Watch your back." And with that, Doris pivoted and went through the jail's back door.

CHAPTER TEN

On the way home, I mulled over Doris's parting shot. Was she trying to get me to stop investigating, or was she just being melodramatic?

Or did she know something that she didn't want to have come out?

That made me stop and think about what impact it would have on Jimmy if he found out Julie had been unfaithful. Then again, the impact of being convicted of her murder would be worse. I didn't know what the exact charges were, but if the prosecution could somehow make a case for premeditation…

I shuddered. Florida is a death-penalty state.

As I pulled up in front of my house, I shook my head to clear it. I'd have to put all these questions on hold for a while. It was time to take Max to Pete Sanchez.

I called Becky to make sure she was available to let Buddy and Lacy out midday for the next few days.

Sergeant Sanchez turned out to be a bit on the stubborn side. I tried very hard not to lock horns directly with him.

But finally on the third morning of his training, I'd had it. "Look, this dog is not an Army raw recruit and he doesn't need strict discipline. He's already highly trained. Can you just show him a little bit of affection so he becomes attached to you?"

Sanchez stared at me for a long, long moment, a vein in his right temple throbbing.

I feared I'd gone too far. "You were nice to him when I introduced you four months ago." It was something Mattie insisted on–make sure the dog and recipient got along well before investing all those hours of training. This time I might have misjudged their compatibility, and that could be an expensive mistake for me. "What happened to the friendly guy who scratched behind his ears?"

We were in the backyard of Sanchez's small rancher on the outskirts of Ocala. He looked away from me, blinking hard. Then he swept his arm in a vague gesture toward the house.

Suddenly, I got it. Keeping my voice gentle, I asked, "Where's your wife?"

He swallowed hard, his Adam's apple bobbing in his neck. "She left. Last week."

My chest ached, with sympathy for the man, but also with guilt. If I'd brought Max to him sooner, would that have given his wife hope that things were going to get better?

It probably wouldn't have made all that much difference. Service dogs weren't the cure-all for PTSD. They only helped to manage the symptoms.

Still, I felt bad. "I'm sorry, Pete. That's gotta be rough."

He nodded, not making eye contact.

"Do you want to call it a day?"

He shook his head. "You drove all the way up here."

It was times like these when my background in human psychology came in handy. The fact that I'd had my own marriage fall apart also helped. I could definitely empathize.

"Let's take a break. Call Max to come and he'll fall in beside you."

Pete looked down at the dog sitting at my feet.

Max was panting due to the warm day, his tongue hanging out of one side of his mouth. Big brown eyes were set against tawny fur. He cocked his head to one side. I wondered if he'd picked up that gesture from Buddy.

"Come, boy," Pete said, his voice much softer than it had

been the last two days.

Max stood and wagged his tail. Pete reached his hand out toward him and Max touched his palm with his nose.

It's progress, I thought as I handed Pete the leash.

Inside, I told Pete to give Max the off-duty signal. He seemed a bit self-conscious doing it, but that's part of the reason for the human phase of the training, to get the owner to the point where the signals are second nature.

We sat down at the kitchen table with glasses of iced tea. Out of deference to me, Pete had made a pitcher of unsweetened.

"It's got to be hard," I said, "to let anybody or anything in right now. But dogs aren't people. They're the most loyal creatures ever. It truly is 'until death do us part' with them."

Pete's grip tightened on his sweating glass of tea but he didn't say anything. Then he looked down at Max and his expression softened.

Pete's training was far from complete, but maybe Max was just what he needed right now. I weighed the pros and cons of what I was considering. Max *was* highly trained and I doubted Pete could undo that in twenty-four hours. I decided to risk it.

"Let's do a little experiment. I'm going to leave Max with you tonight and come back tomorrow afternoon to continue the training. You all can have a little guy time to bond." I winked.

Pete actually smiled. "I guess that'd be good. What do I feed him?"

"I've got some food and treats in the car. I'll get them."

The shortened training day with Pete gave me a free afternoon. I stopped at my house to check on Lacy, then collected Buddy, opting to leave the service vest off today. We headed for Collinsville.

I should have spent the unexpected free time on a training session with Lacy, but I was worried about Jimmy. It had been several days since I'd taken Buddy to see him. Not that the last visit had seemed to cheer him up all that much, but it was all I could do for him at this point. That and keep trying to find out who really killed his wife.

I arrived a little after one-thirty. My stomach growled as I put the car in park in front of the sheriff's department. I wished I'd taken the time to get some lunch.

A few minutes later, I was glad my stomach was empty.

I stepped through the door with Buddy in tow, braced to do battle with Doris, the Defender of the Realm.

But the woman's expression was more sober than sour today. She ducked her head a little when she saw me. "Sheriff Haines will want to speak to you, Ms. Banks. Hold on a sec." Her tone lacked its usual snippy edge.

She disappeared into the sheriff's office, then immediately reappeared. She buzzed me in. "Go on back."

My curiosity about what was going on turned to dread when I saw the sheriff's grim expression.

He stood behind his desk. "Sit down, Ms. Banks."

I sank onto the visitor's chair in front of his desk. Buddy lowered his butt to the floor beside me.

The sheriff scrubbed his face with a big hand. "No good way to say this. I'm afraid Jimmy Garrett is gone."

"Gone?"

Did he escape? I found that hard to believe.

"He's… dead."

My mind blanked, unable to process the information. I'd gone hollow inside. "Dead?"

"Yes, ma'am. He, uh, he killed himself, about two hours ago."

My empty stomach roiled. Bile rose in my throat. I clasped a hand over my mouth.

The sheriff rushed around the desk, then stopped a couple of feet from me. His hands hung at his sides, a look of utter helplessness on his face. Then he gathered himself. "Can I get you something? Some water?"

I shook my head. When I was able to trust that I wouldn't be sick all over his desk, I lowered my hand. "Killed himself? How?"

The sheriff pinched his lips together in a tight line. "He hung himself in the shower, with his jumpsuit. One of my deputies found him when he went in to take him back to his cell."

His tone was angry, but I couldn't tell if he was angry at me or himself. The implication hadn't escaped me. No doubt Jimmy had stood on the shower chair we had so helpfully provided.

I should have brought Buddy sooner. I shook my head, knowing it probably wouldn't have made a difference.

Suddenly the hollowness inside was filled with a leaden pressure. I thought my chest might explode. Tears sprang to my eyes.

"He's dead? You're sure?"

The sheriff nodded, his expression softer now. "We have to send the body to Lakeland for an autopsy, but we do have a local coroner. He's tentatively ruled it was death by asphyxiation."

A sob escaped from my throat.

He awkwardly patted my shoulder. "I'm so sorry," he said in a low voice.

I almost lost it. My survival instincts kicked in. "I've got to go." I jumped up and practically ran from the sheriff's office, Buddy trotting after me.

In the outer waiting area of the station, Buddy stopped. He looked up at me, his head tilted to one side, no doubt wondering why we weren't going back to see Jimmy.

I choked back another sob and moved toward the door.

"Ms. Banks." Doris's raspy voice.

I looked over my shoulder.

The woman's face was unreadable but her shoulders sagged. "I'm sorry. I never meant for this to happen."

I shook my head slightly, then yanked the door open and fled.

I knew I was in no shape to drive so I headed for the small park in the center of town. I sat down on a bench and tried to process what had happened.

How could Jimmy be dead?

Buddy put his head on my knee and whined softly. I absently scratched his ears.

Julie was dead, murdered. Jimmy was dead by his own hand, pushed over the brink by her loss and being jailed for her murder. Ida Mae was an orphan, her only relatives an aunt and uncle who really didn't want her.

Buddy stirred, whined again. I looked down at him. He was an orphan too.

I guess he's mine now.

That thought warmed my chest, but then my gut twisted so bad I doubled over.

No, it wasn't my fault that Jimmy was dead. I'd tried to cheer him up, tried to find out who had framed him for Julie's murder.

And as much as I loved the idea of owning Buddy, I would have preferred the heart-wrenching moment of giving him back to Jimmy over this pain any day of the week.

My throat closed and the tears that had been building in my eyes leaked down my cheeks. I sniffed hard and tried to suck it up before I lost it completely.

Buddy's ears perked. He wagged his tail.

A moment later, a hand squeezed my shoulder.

I jumped, belatedly realizing that Buddy had been signaling someone's approach. My head jerked up.

I gazed into the eyes of the owner of the hand, and lost it completely.

CHAPTER ELEVEN

Through my sobs, it barely registered that Sheriff Haines had settled onto the bench beside me, and that Buddy had offered no protest to this.

Indeed, Buddy transferred his head from my knee to the sheriff's khaki-covered one and whined. The sheriff patted his head with one hand.

His other arm settled around my shaking shoulders. I turned my head against his chest and cried harder.

I started blubbering about how I should have done more for Jimmy. I didn't know half of what I was saying, nor why. "It's all my fault. I failed him. I'm a failure."

"You didn't fail him. You're the one who believed in him when everybody else was convinced he was guilty."

"You don't understand," I wailed. "He was my first one. My first big success, and now he's dead."

"Ah, so this isn't about Jimmy," the sheriff said.

I pulled back from him. "How can you say that? Of course, this is about Jimmy."

He shook his head. "Grief is never just about the person who's gone. It's about what their loss means to us."

That stopped me cold. I digested his words as I dug in my purse, found a tissue and blew my nose.

With a start, I realized he was right. I gave him a sideways glance. "How'd you get to be so smart about such things?"

"Bachelor's in criminal justice, with a psych minor." He

looked away, jaw clenched. "Grief, it's a bugger to deal with."

He turned back toward me and his face softened. "So Jimmy was your first big success story. What's happened here recently doesn't change that."

It was my turn to look away. "He was doing so well."

"Yeah, pretty well. He couldn't seem to find himself in terms of a job. But he and Julie both seemed okay with him being a stay-at-home dad. She had a good income and was about to get her inheritance. They would have been fine…" His voice trailed off.

I knew the statistics. The suicide rate amongst veterans of the Iraqi and Afghanistan wars was fifty percent higher than the general public's. Yes, he'd seemed to be doing fine, but who knew how firm his grasp on okayness had really been, even before Julie's murder?

"They were good people," I said softly.

"They were. Better than some around here."

I looked up at the bright blue sky, blinking back fresh tears. It wasn't right that it was so sunny. Surely gray clouds should be hanging low on such a day.

"It's not right," I whispered.

His jaw clenched again. "No, it's not." He meant something else entirely.

Suddenly I felt an overwhelming urge to get out of Collinsville. The air, even the sunshine there, felt toxic.

I mumbled a goodbye to the sheriff and headed in the direction of my car. Twenty or so feet away from the bench, I heard him call out. "Ms. Banks, you gonna be okay?"

I turned back toward him and nodded, unable to trust my voice.

"Can I call you in a day or two? You know, to check on you?"

I nodded again and hurried across the park.

I was almost to my car when another voice called my name. "Ms. Banks, or should I say Mrs. Goldman!"

I looked up.

John Collins was bearing down on me, his face thunderous.

Even though he was off duty, Buddy stepped in front of me. I tightened my hold on his leash, but I didn't give him the *friend* signal. The anger radiating off Collins made my stomach clench.

The man abruptly stopped a few feet away. "I understand you questioned my wife."

I raised my eyebrows at him. I couldn't think of a thing to say that wouldn't sound defensive so I said nothing.

Collins took a step toward me.

A low rumbling in Buddy's throat. This time I didn't blame him for breaking training. I wanted to growl at Collins myself.

"Sit." But I still withheld the *friend* signal.

Buddy complied, the hair bristling on his neck.

Good boy, I thought silently.

"Look, we've got enough grief in this town right now," Collins said. "We don't need you pokin' around, stickin' your nose in where it don't belong."

Doris was right. It didn't take much to scratch away the sophisticated veneer and expose the Florida cracker underneath.

"Jimmy Garrett murdered my sister, and he's gonna pay for it–"

"That's enough!" The sheriff's voice barked from behind me.

Collins looked over my shoulder. He puffed out his chest. "You talkin' to me, Sheriff?" His voice was belligerent.

"Yes, I am."

Collins' hands went to his hips. "I can't say that I care for your tone."

"That makes two of us. Leave Ms. Banks alone."

"You seem to be forgetting something, Sheriff." Collins circled around me.

I pivoted. Buddy angled himself between me and the two men who were now just a couple of feet apart, leaning into each other's faces.

"I can ruin you, Haines," Collins hissed in a low voice.

"Maybe, maybe not, but I'll not have you harassing innocent bystanders."

Collins snorted loudly. "Innocent? Her? She's been talking to people all over town, stirring up trouble. Came into the bank and pretended she was someone she ain't."

"Last I checked we still have freedom of speech in this country," the sheriff replied. "Now why don't you go on about your business?"

"I'll worry about my business and you worry about yours." Collins narrowed his eyes. "If you expect to get re-elected, you'd better come up with enough evidence to convict Jimmy Garrett. He's gonna fry for my sister's murder."

"Afraid not."

Collins faced turned even uglier. "What the devil do ya mean by that?"

"You haven't heard?" the sheriff said conversationally. "Jimmy Garrett's dead."

Collins deflated like a popped balloon. His shoulders fell and his face sagged. "Dead?"

"Killed himself."

Collins' mouth fell open. Then he closed it and whirled toward me. "Then you got no more business around here, missy. Get out of my town."

The sheriff stepped around him. "You've got no authority to order anyone out of this town, Collins." He reached for my elbow. "Ms. Banks, may I walk you to your car?"

I managed a slight nod of my head. We started down the sidewalk, Buddy beside me, Collins sputtering behind us.

His shoe scraped on the concrete. Buddy whirled around.

Collins had the good sense to stop moving. He glared at me one last time, then pivoted and marched away.

I held my hand out toward Buddy, palm down. "It's okay, boy." He touched his nose to my hand and gave a tentative wag of his tail.

At my car, I fumbled some with my key fob. Finally I managed to hit the button and unlock the doors.

The sheriff leaned down to grab the driver's door handle.

"I need to put Buddy in the back."

"Oh, sure. Sorry." He opened the back door instead.

Once I had Buddy attached to his safety harness, I pulled my head out of the backseat area and started to open my door.

Will Haines put a gentle hand on my arm. "You did everything you could for Jimmy. Wish I could say the same."

His words hit me like a brick between the eyes. Of course he would be feeling awful about Jimmy's suicide.

"It's not your fault," I said.

"It sure is. Happened on my watch. And we're supposed to keep an eye out for that kind of thing." He shook his head. "You even pointed out to me that he was down."

"Still, I didn't think he was suicidal."

He shook his head again. "Drive careful going home."

"I will."

He turned and walked away. I watched his broad back, wishing there was something I could say that would make him feel better.

I'd planned to go on home, but when I started the engine and pulled away from the curb, the car perversely headed toward Jimmy's street. Tears sprang to my eyes again as I cruised past the sad little house.

The curtain in the front window next door fluttered.

I pulled over and stopped the car.

I faked another sip of sweet tea and hoped Miss Shirley wouldn't notice that the volume of liquid in my glass hadn't gone down any. Buddy sat quietly at my feet, panting softly.

I had just scored mega brownie points by bringing her the news that Jimmy was dead. I hated to use the information in such a gossipy way, but if it helped me find Julie's killer, I figured Jimmy would forgive me.

Amazingly, Miss Shirley hadn't heard about it yet.

It crossed my mind, too late, that the sheriff might be sitting on that news for some reason. But he'd probably assume Miss

Shirley got it out of one of the deputies or from John Collins. He wouldn't suspect me since he thought I was headed home.

And I was, just as soon as I pumped this woman for more information.

"Miss Shirley, I know you said you didn't see the person who was sneaking in the back next door, but maybe you know more than you think you do. Maybe there was something you heard or an impression of the person's size?"

"I did hear what sounded like Doris's voice a couple of times. But I figured I was mishearin' it. That it was really a man's voice. 'Cause why would Doris come around back like that? She didn't need to sneak in."

"Well, it is a rural town," I said. "Don't lots of people use their back door all the time, even for visitors?"

Miss Shirley set her glass down on a crocheted coaster. "Not when the backyard's fenced in like theirs is, and the front door is right there by the street. Why, even Jimmy and Julie came and went through the front."

I nodded. "How about the height of the person? You saw flashes of tan. How far up on the bushes was that? Around your eye level? Or lower, higher?"

She closed her eyes. After a moment, she opened them again and held her hand at mid-chest level. "About here, I think. Coulda been somebody's work pants."

Miss Shirley was maybe an inch taller than my five-five, and willowly thin to the point of looking frail. So mid chest on her could be the pants of a large man or the shirt of an average man or woman. Not all that helpful, really.

"The morning that Julie died," I said, "did you see or hear anything then?" I was pretty sure we'd already covered this, but they were always saying on cop shows that people sometimes remembered stuff later.

"I did hear raised voices over there, early that mornin'. Then Julie closed the bedroom window and I couldn't hear them no more."

"Raised voices as in yelling?"

"No, just talkin' loud, kinda angry. But I couldn't make out what they were sayin'."

"Were they Jimmy's and Julie's voices?"

Miss Shirley paused, then shook her head. "I did hear Julie clear for a moment when she came over and slammed the window shut, but the other voice was only a rumble."

"But you didn't see anybody coming or going out back that day?"

"No, but then I was weedin' my front flower beds that mornin'. I wasn't around back much. Just to get my gloves and hat outta the shed."

"Did you tell the sheriff about the voices?"

She nodded. "Frank Larson interviewed me. He wrote it all down in that little note pad of his and said he'd tell the sheriff everything I said."

"Do you have any clue who might have called in that anonymous tip? Sheriff Haines assumed it was you."

She shook her head rather vehemently. "I ain't got no reason to call nothin' in anonymously. I would've identified myself."

That I believed!

I thanked Miss Shirley and said my goodbyes.

She gestured toward Buddy, a nonverbal request to pet him. I was impressed. All too many people didn't get it that one couldn't interact with a service dog the same way you would with someone's pet.

I nodded and she patted Buddy on the head. "Guess I won't be seeing you again."

His tail wagged vigorously.

My assessment of Miss Shirley went up several more notches. If Buddy liked her, she couldn't be that bad.

Once outside, I led Buddy next door to Jimmy and Julie's property. Their corner lot was probably close to a half acre. A tall wooden, privacy fence, like the one around my own yard–they're quite common in Florida–ran down the left side and across the back of the property. It looked new, the wood not yet faded.

I located the gate along the side. Testing the latch, I discovered it wasn't locked. Buddy and I slipped through the gate, then I closed it behind us.

The yard was cluttered with the paraphernalia of a young family's life–a gas grill, a wooden picnic table, a coil of garden hose. One grassy area was dedicated to outdoor toddler-sized toys, including a small wading pool. The water in it had turned slimy.

A wave of sadness washed over me. The Garretts would never again grill hamburgers and sit at that picnic table to eat them. My mind conjured up an image of a carefree version of the solemn toddler I'd seen at the Collins' house, splashing in that wading pool. I swallowed hard.

Then I shook my head. I hadn't come back here to wallow in grief. I walked around the yard for a couple of minutes, Buddy keeping pace with me.

Azalea bushes higher than my head grew along the right side of the yard abutting Miss Shirley's property. Between the foliage, I could make out a chainlink fence behind them, and the occasional glimpse of Miss Shirley's yard.

She hadn't been lying about the thickness of the bushes. There was no way she'd be able to see much through them.

Considering her nosy temperament, it was quite likely the Garretts, and probably Julie's grandparents before them, had left the bushes that way on purpose.

I turned Buddy loose to go sniff and mark some of those bushes. Then I climbed up the two steps to the poured-concrete back porch. It ran the length of the house, with an old-fashioned aluminum awning providing some shade.

I peered in the kitchen window. The kitchen was tidy. Two coffee mugs rested upside down in the dish drainer next to the sink under the window. The room looked perfectly normal and yet I had a niggling feeling that something was off about it. I bracketed the sides of my face with my hands, blocking out the sunlight, and scanned the room again.

When my gaze fell on the coffee mugs, I got it. There were traces of lipstick and dried drops of coffee on them. Someone had put them in the drainer without actually washing them.

I glanced at the refrigerator across the room, which reminded me of the beer. Jimmy had claimed there was no beer in the house, and the sheriff had confirmed that. Had someone brought beer with them into the house and poured it over him while he was knocked out cold? That smacked of premeditation, that the killer had planned to murder Julie and frame Jimmy for it.

But how could someone count on being able to get the drop on Jimmy? He was an ex-Marine and he ran daily. Not an easy person to bring down.

A more likely scenario was that Jimmy came home before the killer had been able to get away, and conking him on the head was a spontaneous act of desperation.

Which brought me back to where the heck did the beer come from.

Buddy woofed at me from the yard, then jumped up on the porch beside me and nudged a cold nose against my palm.

"Would you have let someone pour beer over your unconscious owner?" I asked him.

He tilted his head to one side, looking for all the world like he was contemplating the question.

Maybe he would, if he thought the person was there to help his owner.

I tested the back door and wasn't surprised to find it locked.

Figuring the house and yard had told me all they could, I hooked Buddy's leash to his collar and led him out of the side gate.

We rounded the corner, headed for my car. I jerked to a stop. A sheriff's department cruiser was parked across the street from the Garretts' front door, with Frank Larson at the wheel.

I studiously ignored the deputy as I loaded Buddy into my car, climbed in and drove away.

Why was he there? Did he happen to be in the neighborhood? Had Will Haines sent him to look out for me? Or to spy on me?

The Garrett house had long since been cleared as a crime scene, and the owners were hardly in a position to report me for trespassing.

Wait, who would be the owner now? John Collins, I supposed. Yeah, he would report me. But how would he know I was poking around?

I shrugged off these futile musings and turned my mind to what I was going to do with all this.

Despite the sheriff's sympathy and his own feelings of guilt, I doubted he would continue to work to clear Jimmy's name. The victim was dead; the accused was dead. Case closed.

But somehow I couldn't let the world continue to believe that Jimmy Garrett was a murderer. And especially, I felt I owed it to that little girl to clear her father's name and bring her mother's killer to justice.

So what did I have?

John Collins wanted me to butt out. Understandable in a way. His sister had been killed. He was convinced Jimmy was the killer. He didn't want me clouding the issue.

Maybe my visit had upset his wife more than she'd let on. And he probably didn't like the fact that I'd made a fool of him, pretending to be a potential rich customer.

Frank Larson? He was a big guy. The flashes of tan Miss Shirley saw in the Garretts' backyard could have been his uniform. The voice she'd heard occasionally could have been his. Maybe he had been Julie's lover. His big belly said he probably drank beer on a regular basis and might have some handy to pour on Jimmy.

I had trouble imagining Julie being attracted to Deputy Frank, but there was no accounting for some people's tastes.

Again, something was niggling at the back of my brain. I tried to capture the thought but it kept slithering away.

I was close to home when it snuck up on me and pounced. I almost drove off the road.

Doris had said, *I never meant for this to happen*, or words to that effect. Had she been in on the frame?

Doris was wearing long sleeves that morning, in an overly warm building. Were they hiding scratches or bite marks on her arms from where she'd wrestled Buddy out of the way to get to an unconscious Jimmy? Did one of those long sleeves have a tear in it?

Another piece clicked into place.

The two coffee mugs in the dish drainer. They'd *both* had traces of lipstick on them, in two different shades.

CHAPTER TWELVE

I needed to talk to Doris again, but it would have to wait. I had to find out how Pete Sanchez and Max were getting along, and then get back up to Ocala to finish Pete's training.

When I got home, I called Pete. He reported that he and Max were "bonding." I could see him in my mind's eye, making air quotes as he lobbed the psychobabble back at me. We set a time for the next afternoon for a training session.

Then it occurred to me to call Jimmy's former counselor, Jo Ann Hamilton. I doubted anyone else would let her know what had happened. And to be honest, I was a little pissed at her, which wasn't all that reasonable. Obviously she couldn't drop everything in her busy life and go over to Collinsville to see Jimmy in jail.

Or maybe she had, but it hadn't helped all that much. Therapists weren't miracle workers after all.

As the phone rang in my ear, I realized I was really trying to spread the guilt around. I almost hung up.

I actually got Ms. Hamilton this time, live. Now that was a small miracle. And she couldn't have been nicer.

She thanked me again for letting her know about Jimmy's predicament–odd word choice, I thought, but then what else might one call it–and told me that she had been able to talk to him a couple of times on the phone.

"How's he doing?" she asked.

Not knowing how to dress it up, I blurted out that Jimmy had committed suicide.

A sharp intake of air. “Oh, my,” she whispered.

The next thing I knew I was blathering about how it was all my fault because I’d gotten him the shower chair. She pointed out that we are not responsible for other people’s decisions or actions. Something I already knew, of course, but the reminder was much needed. By the time I got off the phone I had an appointment with her for a week from Monday.

I knew it was closing in on that time of the month when I woke up the next morning craving red meat. Normally I’m a chicken and seafood kind of girl. But not today.

I pulled a steak out of the freezer. I’d bought it on sale during my last major shopping run to the nearest Publix, just south of Ocala.

It was huge. I’d get two meals out of it at least. I put the package on top of a paper towel on the counter to defrost (I know, you’re supposed to put it in the fridge, but that never works for me. It’s always still rock solid at dinnertime.)

Then I sat down at my kitchen table with my breakfast and my laptop to catch up on my email. In addition to some business related stuff, there was a message from my mom and, much to my surprise, one from Sheriff Haines. I opened that one first.

Ms. Banks, I wanted to reassure you that I am still checking things out regarding the Garrett case, and you and Buddy are welcome to stop by whenever you’re in the area. Will Haines

Hmm, that was interesting, since John Collins had told me point blank to stay out of *his* town. Apparently, the sheriff had a different idea about whose town it was, and when a murder case would be considered closed. But why was he now encouraging me to come around when he’d warned me before to stop poking my “cute, freckled nose” into things?

I pondered that while dashing off a reply to my mom’s one-line message, *Are you still alive?*

I’d come up with no ideas as to why the good sheriff had sent me that message, so I took care of the business-related stuff.

Nope, still no answer to the burning question regarding Will Haines. Was his message nothing but a macho response, a pissing match between him and Julie's brother over who was going to call the shots in Collinsville? The only other thing that came to mind was that the sheriff liked me and wanted to see me again.

Crapola! He likes me.

I had sworn off men after my disastrous marriage, and I'd been reasonably content with my single status. Relationships were a complication I could do without.

But now…

I decided to do a Scarlett O'Hara and think about it later. Maybe I'd bring it up next week with my new counselor.

My stomach clenched.

Or maybe not. Was I ready to talk about my ambivalence toward men? I shook my head.

For now, it was time to put in some much-needed training with Lacy. I got in a solid hour with her, then took a short break, during which I again contemplated the sheriff's email and Lacy did what dogs do best–sleep.

When we got back to it, Buddy was once again very helpful. He and I demonstrated the desired behavior while Lacy watched. She was a truly smart dog. She'd caught on quickly that if she did what Buddy did, she'd get treats. But that didn't mean we were done. The behaviors had to become second nature to her.

Once his demos were done, Buddy loafed in the shade, his big black head resting on his front paws. But Lacy and I were both overheated by the time I decided I needed to stop, grab some lunch and a quick shower, and then get on the road to Pete Sanchez's house.

I paused on the deck to give Lacy a vigorous head rub and scratch behind her soft ears. "You are such a good girl," I cooed as I released her leash from her service halter, signaled she was off duty, then pulled open the back door.

Buddy sniffed the air and bolted into the house. More odd behavior. I made a mental note to do some refresher training with him soon. Lacy followed him at a more lady-like pace. They both disappeared into the living room.

I paused at the fridge to grab some water. My hand had just wrapped around the cool bottle when the dogs went ballistic.

Dropping the water bottle, I raced into the living room, and froze.

There was an alligator in my house.

CHAPTER THIRTEEN

The gator was only about four feet long. Not a full grown adult, but still quite dangerous. Its big tail thrashed around, sending small pieces of furniture flying. It watched Buddy with beady eyes.

"Back, Buddy!"

He obeyed, moving further away from those scary jaws, but he continued to bark and growl at the intruder.

Lacy huddled in the back corner of her crate. Dogs instinctively "go to ground" when threatened, and domesticated ones considered their crates their dens. So Lacy had assumed that was the safest place to be.

And hopefully she was right. The gator's jaws probably wouldn't fit through the open crate door. A very good thing, since her fifty-pound, delicately framed body was the perfect size for a gator snack.

Buddy was a different matter. Apparently he was big enough to give the gator pause.

The creature backed up into a corner. *Not* a good thing. A cornered animal was doubly dangerous.

My heart, which I swear had stopped beating completely for a few seconds, was now pounding in my chest. I was trying not to hyperventilate. My mind scrambled for a way to get the gator out of my house without injury to me or my dogs.

I flashed to the steak defrosting on the counter. I raced toward the kitchen. It was hard leaving the dogs in the same room with that creature, but I had a half-baked plan.

Ripping the wrapper off the steak, I pulled a long-handled grilling fork out of a drawer and jammed the half-frozen meat onto the tongs.

The nonstop barking told me Buddy was still alive. But I had no idea where the gator was, so I edged around the corner.

The gator snapped his jaws. Buddy jumped back, but it was a near miss. The gator hadn't lunged though. He seemed to still be assessing whether he should take on an eighty–pound, snarling dog.

"Back, Buddy!" I waved the steak in the air, hoping the gator could smell it.

Buddy continued barking, but he backed up until he was next to Lacy's crate.

I waved the steak again. "Come here, Mr. Gator. I've got a snack for you."

The critter seemed to have heard me, or else the odor of raw meat had finally registered in his lizard brain. He turned his head in my direction, his beady eyes glinting in the afternoon sunshine streaming through the living room window.

He took a tentative step in my direction.

Buddy was still barking.

"Quiet, Buddy." It was a risk. If the gator no longer saw Buddy as an ominous foe, he might go after him. But I didn't want his pea brain distracted at this point.

"Come on, Mr. Gator." I waved the steak again.

Suddenly the gator was lunging in my direction.

"Stay, Buddy!" I yelled over my shoulder as I bolted through the kitchen. I never ran so fast in my life, straight out the backdoor, leaving it open.

Thrashing sounds behind me and the rattle of my breakfast dishes still sitting on the table. I didn't turn around to look. I dropped the steak and fork on the deck and kept going.

The gator might be after the meat, or he might be after me at this point. If you got gators pissed off enough, they'd attack even adults.

I wasn't taking any chances.

At the gate in the privacy fence, I fumbled with the clip I used to keep it from being opened from the outside. Thank the good Lord I'd never gotten around to replacing the clip with a padlock as I'd originally intended.

The thrashing sounds had stopped. I took a quick look over my shoulder and thought I glanced gator green through the branches of the camellia bush between me and the deck. Still too close for comfort.

For a second the animal lover in me worried about the gator getting the fork stuck in his jaws.

Get a grip, Banks!

Once through the gate, I debated about leaving it open so the gator could get out on his own if he so chose. But then there was a risk Lacy would get out as well, since both her crate and the back door were hanging open.

The deciding factor was the thought that if I left it open, I wouldn't know for sure where the gator was. If I came back and the creature was gone, I wouldn't know if he'd left through the gate or had gone back into the house.

An image of the gator slithering out from under my bed in the middle of the night popped into my mind. I shuddered even though that scenario was highly unlikely. If the gator ended up back in the house, he was more likely to show himself and take off a limb or two long before bedtime.

I shoved the gate closed and ran around the house. My brain desperately searched for a way to get Buddy out of harm's way. But the front door was locked, and I didn't have my keys on me. And I wasn't about to return to that backyard to check out the status of Mr. Gator.

I ran like a crazy woman toward the Mayfair Motel.

Dexter Mayfair, Edna's great-nephew and old man Mayfair's grandson, wasn't the sharpest knife in the drawer, but he'd inherited the Mayfair way with animals, especially reptiles.

He was our local go-to person when a gator showed up where it didn't belong.

"Aw, Marcia," Dexter yelled from the living room. "He's jest a young un."

"Is Buddy okay?" I called out from my spot on the deck. I was under strict orders to stay put.

"I don't see him."

My heart stopped.

"Wait, he's under the couch," Dexter called out.

My chest swelled with parental pride–that was one smart dog–even as my brain struggled with the logistics of an eighty-pound dog getting under a couch that was five inches off the floor.

The living room erupted in snapping and thrashing sounds. I prayed like crazy that the sounds were the gator fighting the big stick thingie with the loop on the end that Dexter carried, and not the gator eating Dexter or one of the dogs.

Dexter also had a pistol with him. "Tranquilizer darts," he'd huffed out as we'd run from the motel back to my house.

More thrashing. Dexter was still alive. I could hear him cursing a blue streak.

"Get outta the way. I'm bringing him out!"

I was in the middle of my backyard before I had time to think. My feet had apparently processed Dexter's words faster than my brain had.

The gate! I ran to open it just as Dexter backed out the back door, a thrashing mass of lizard on the other end of the loop thingie, which was now firmly attached to the gator's jaws. My bistro table went flying.

I threw the gate open, then ran to Dexter's truck at the curb in front of my house. I didn't want to be anywhere near that creature.

But by the time Dexter came through the gate, he was practically dragging the gator behind him. "Tranq I shot him with finally took hold," Dexter said through huffs and puffs of exertion. "Don't like to tranq 'em lest I have to. But I didn't want him gettin' ahold of one of yer dogs."

"Thanks so much, Dexter!"

I was practically in tears. Now that the danger was over, my knees turned to jelly. I grabbed for the truck's door handle to hold myself up.

A soft woof came from the backyard.

Crapola! How could I forget the dogs?

I raced back around the corner of the house. Buddy was standing in the gate opening, a flash of Lacy's white tail behind him.

Sinking to my knees beside the big black dog, I threw my arms around him and sobbed out my relief.

CHAPTER FOURTEEN

My hands were still shaking as I attempted to sip from the cup of mint tea that Edna Mayfair had insisted on making for me. The dogs lay on the floor, my own and Edna's two Springer Spaniels, Benny and Bo. The "boys," as Edna called them, were panting loudly after having spent the better part of five minutes yapping and running in excited circles around Buddy and Lacy. Buddy had looked at me. When I shook my head, he ignored them.

Lacy had started to respond with some yips of her own and a wagging rear-end, but I'd ordered her to lie down. I was quite gratified, and a little surprised, when she'd complied. Despite all the upheaval lately, she was coming along.

Edna had finally been able to quiet her dogs. Now she sat across from me, in one of her bright colored muumuus, and slowly shook her head. White wisps of hair fluffed out from her head, stirred by the breeze from the boxy air conditioner chugging away behind her in the kitchen window.

Central air had been a newfangled thing when the Mayfair Motel was built. Edna, the old man's sister, had run it from the get-go. Rumor had it that she'd socked away a small fortune during the brief heyday of the Mayfair Alligator Farm. Obviously she hadn't invested much of that fortune in upkeep. Now, the motel subsisted on lunchtime trysts and construction workers brought in to build things in the larger towns in the area. Edna's ability to offer cut-rate lodgings–since she'd long since paid off the mortgage on her land–made the Mayfair far more cost-effective than the motels in those bigger towns.

"How long have ya lived down here now?" Edna said. "Doncha know better than to leave yer doors hangin' open, no matter how nice the day is?"

Both were rhetorical questions. Edna had personally taken me under her wing when I'd moved to town and filled me in on the main rule of living in rural Florida. Never leave an unscreened window or door open, even in what passes for winter down here. This was to prevent snakes and insects and the small lizards that were everywhere down here from getting into your house. Gators with wanderlust were a rarity, unless you had a pool or a pond on your property. But even then, they didn't come in the house!

"I didn't leave a door open," I said.

"Must have."

I took a swig of tea, the mint tangy on my tongue, and shook my head. "I don't know how the gator got in."

Dexter saved me from further interrogation by coming into the kitchen, the screen door banging closed behind him.

Lacy jumped up and woofed. I held a hand out, palm parallel with the floor. "Down."

She immediately dropped down again, but she watched Dexter warily. Was she associating him with the gator?

I reached down and scratched behind her ears. "It's okay, girl."

"I gotta take that youngster out into the Forest 'fore he wakes up," Dexter said, "but I wanted to let you know you could go back into yer house now, Marcia. I checked all the walls, inside and out. Couldn't find no holes he could've gotten in through. Ya musta left a door open."

I stifled the urge to sigh. I knew I hadn't. I kept the front door locked. The only person who had a key was Becky, who knew better than to let a dog get past her.

The back screen door had one of those automatic closer thingies and I was pretty sure I'd heard it slam shut behind us when Buddy, Lacy and I had gone out back for our last training session. And while we were in the backyard, I'm darn sure I would've noticed a gator slither by, headed for the house.

Besides, how would he have gotten into the fenced backyard to begin with? I made a mental note to check the fence for holes. Could he have been hiding under a bush somewhere out there?

Again, unlikely, but gators didn't teleport themselves into houses. He'd had to have gotten in there somehow.

"Thanks a million, Dexter," I said. "I don't know what I would've done without you."

He ducked his head. "S'okay. Happy to help out. Uh, your livin' room's kinda busted up, just ta warn you."

This time I let the sigh escape. "I figured it would be. Guess I'd better go start the clean up. Hopefully the gator didn't poop in there."

Dexter made eye contact for a brief moment and grinned. "Don't think so. Didn't smell nothin' but swamp slime."

I tried to return his smile but I suspect it was more of a grimace. "Thank God for small favors."

Two hours later, I had called Pete Sanchez to reschedule our training session for the next morning–he totally understood when he heard the reason–and I had most of the mess squared away. A pile of broken pieces of wood outside the front door represented the remains of one of the end tables. The shattered lamp from the latter was in the trash can. I'd managed to glue together my grandmother's piecrust-top, antique tea table. It was perched precariously in one corner while the glue dried. The gator had also taken out a back leg of the cushioned armchair. A pile of old textbooks sufficed as a crutch. There were dark smudges of mud on the sofa, but upholstery cleaner would likely get those out.

I was mopping up mud from the terrazzo floor when it truly hit me–what I'd known in the back of my mind all along. Somebody had to have put that gator in here on purpose. I sat down abruptly on the sofa and shook my head, trying to dislodge the thought. Was I being paranoid?

But there really wasn't any way the creature could've gotten into the house under its own steam.

My heart raced. I didn't know anyone sick enough to think a gator in one's living room would make a good practical joke, and the only enemy that immediately came to mind was my ex. But he had no reason to come after me at this point. Besides it would never occur to him to use a gator to try to take me out.

It was a sloppy and unreliable way to kill someone anyway.

But maybe death hadn't been the intention. Maybe the gator was meant to be a distraction. Or a warning.

I pulled out my cell phone. I had no enemies in Mayfair or Ocala, but Collinsville was another story. The sheriff's department phone was ringing when I disconnected.

Will Haines was going to think I was nuts. Maybe he'd be more willing to believe me if I talked to him in person.

I contemplated that as I went out back and righted my bistro table. It was a little bent but only slightly wobbly. I put it back on the deck and retrieved the least mangled of the chairs. I sat down.

The thought of staring across the sheriff's desk into his big blue eyes made my nether regions tingle, even as my stomach clenched.

Crapola! I like him too.

Should I call for an appointment?

I wanted to talk to Doris again, and I didn't particularly want to give her any warning. Also, it wouldn't be good if word got out that I was coming, and maybe found its way to the person or persons responsible for the giant reptile in my living room. Might be better to just show up.

I noticed a twisted piece of metal, with something orange on one end, lying in the grass. What the heck was that?

I stood and walked over to scoop the object up. The University of Florida logo–a gator head–grinned at me from the remains of the grilling fork's orange plastic handle. I shuddered.

I would take the fork with me to show to the sheriff. Maybe then he'd take me seriously.

CHAPTER FIFTEEN

Needless to say, I didn't sleep well that night.

I was feeling a bit desperate about getting to Collinsville to talk to the sheriff. I wanted someone to be aware of my suspicions, just in case I turned up dead from some freak accident. Not that the sheriff knowing it wasn't an accident would help me much at that point. I think I was harboring some unrealistic fantasy that he would now be able to magically solve Julie's murder, and I would then be safe.

But first I had to meet my obligations to my trainees. Most of the following day I spent with Pete Sanchez and Max. They now seemed to be hitting it off, and Pete was in a better mood. We made a lot of progress. After a short debate with myself, I decided to leave Max with him. We made an appointment for me to return in two days.

After a quick stop at the Home Depot in Ocala, I headed home to work with Lacy. I'd contemplated putting that off for a day and going to Collinsville. But she'd been upset by the gator incident and I wanted to get her mind back on business.

And it was Sunday. I had no idea how to discreetly find Sheriff Haines if he wasn't at the sheriff's department.

No great progress was made with Lacy but she did seem to be back on track. I cut the session a little short because I was anxious to install my hardware purchases–dead bolt locks for both doors and two battery-operated gizmos that made an obnoxious noise when the magnetic connection was broken between the sensor on the door and the one on the doorjamb. A poor woman's alarm system.

Buddy and Lacy went berserk when I tested it. "Sorry," I said as I hastily closed the door again, then reached up to flip the switch to the off position.

I wondered if I was over-reacting. The dogs were my four-legged alarm system. Why did I need anything else? My mind flashed to Lacy alone in her crate tomorrow while I was in Collinsville. I shuddered at the thought of someone breaking in and harming her, and/or leaving some new reptilian guest to greet me when I got home.

Maybe I should spring for a real alarm system, complete with monitoring. I shook my head. I couldn't afford that. Hopefully, the obnoxious noise would give an intruder pause.

Bright and early the next morning, Buddy and I headed for Collinsville. We got there at nine-thirty, but Doris informed me that the sheriff was out of the office.

"When will he be back?" I said from the other side of the counter.

"Not sure. He had to go out to the Turners' place." She didn't elaborate further.

The ancient air conditioner rumbled in the distance, with little positive results. The air in the outer office area was downright muggy. I noticed that Doris was wearing short sleeves today.

"What's that?" She pointed to the twisted fork in my hand.

I grimaced. "Long story." I considered telling her, while watching her reactions. Would she be truly shocked?

But telling her probably meant telling the whole town, and I didn't want that just yet. Not until I'd talked to the sheriff about it.

She absentmindedly scratched the inside of one wrist. "You can wait if you like. Over there." She swung her arm out toward a few metal chairs lined up along one wall.

Her scratching had left red marks on her wrist. I wondered if she'd picked up some poison ivy somewhere. Or maybe she was allergic to mosquito bites, like Becky was. She got welts the size of fifty-cent pieces from the little buggers.

It took a beat for Buddy's low growl to register over the rumble of the air conditioner.

I glanced down. *What the…?*

His lips were curled back from his teeth. Another low growl.

I put my hand on his head.

His lips uncurled but he kept his gaze on Doris.

I looked up at her. Her eyes had gone wide. She covered her wrist with her other hand.

Pieces fell into place with a mental ka-ching. I reached across the counter and grabbed her arm.

She tried to yank away from me, her body jerking off of her stool. I hung on.

Buddy growled louder. I'd inadvertently loosened my grip on his leash. He came up on his back legs and landed his front paws on the counter.

Doris pulled back as far as she could. She almost lifted me off my feet as my arm and torso stretched across the counter top. But I wasn't letting go.

"Down, Buddy!" I ordered.

He dropped his paws to the floor but continued to growl.

I tugged her arm toward me so I could get a better look. Sure enough there was the yellow of fading bruises and several pinkish-brown spots, new skin healed over puncture wounds.

"That's a dog bite, isn't it, Doris?"

"How'd he recognize it?" Her voice quavered.

"He didn't. Your arm gesture triggered his memory. You tried to hold him off, or maybe hit him? That morning at Julie's house."

"No. He came at me. I just put my arm up, to protect myself."

"And he bit you. Why? Had he seen you hurt Julie?"

"No, no!" She yanked hard, got her arm free. She backed up three paces and dropped her face into her hands, sobbing.

I reached for the door between the lobby and the inner sanctum. It was locked, of course.

"Buzz me in, Doris. This is not a conversation you want someone walking in on. Especially not the sheriff."

A small voice in my head said, *Are you nuts? She could be armed.*

I didn't think she was. And I didn't want to lose my advantage. With no time to think, she might reveal more than she otherwise would.

"Keep that dog away from me."

"I will. He's well trained. He won't hurt you unless I tell him to." Actually, he wouldn't hurt her even if I did tell him to–he wasn't an attack dog–but she didn't know that.

Surprisingly, she reached under the counter and hit the buzzer. I pushed through the door, Buddy on my heels. Grabbing her arm, I hustled her toward the cell area.

"So you didn't hurt Julie, but you hit Jimmy," I said as we went. I made it a statement, even though it was only a guess.

She was crying into her hands again. Her head bobbed in a nod.

In the hallway between the cells, I stopped and turned her toward me. "Why'd you hit him?"

She raised her head. Her mascara had run, giving her a raccoon look. "I panicked. Julie and I'd been fighting." She rubbed an arm across her wet face, smearing the mascara even worse. "Not physically. Arguing, I mean. The front door opened and I panicked. He was walkin' toward the kitchen. I ran out and hit him from behind, with a vase from the cabinet by the door."

I shook my head. This didn't make a whole lot of sense. "Why?" I said again.

"I thought she was going to tell him right then."

"Tell him what?"

Her face flushed red. I figured it out half a second before she said it. "About us."

"You were the one having an affair with her."

She suddenly stood up straighter. "If you tell the sheriff, I'll deny it."

I grabbed her arm and shook her. Buddy whimpered softly, not sure what was going on.

"Tell me all of it. Then I'll decide who I'm gonna tell what." My voice was harsh in my ears. Fury churned in my stomach. Two good people had died to keep this woman's little secret.

Doris must have read the rage in my face. Her eyes went even wider. "I didn't kill Julie. I swear it! And I didn't set Jimmy up. I just hit him and then… I left."

"Tell me," I said through gritted teeth. "From the beginning."

"Julie and I had been friends for a long time. She didn't know how I felt about her." The words tumbled out. "Not until she came back here to live with her grandma while Jimmy was overseas. My feelin's got the better of me one day and I kissed her. And then she kissed me back." Doris choked on a half sob. "She ended it when Jimmy came home, but we stayed friends. It was awkward for a while, but finally things kinda went back to normal."

She swiped her arm across her cheek again. "Then she got a case of the guilts. She wanted to tell Jimmy, said it didn't feel right keepin' it from him. That's what we were arguin' about. No tellin' how he'd take it. He might not keep it a secret, and I'd lose my job."

Something exploded in my chest. "All this over a lousy job," I yelled in her face.

"It's not just any job." She turned her head away, but I still had a hold on her arm. I shook it.

"It's an important job," she said, her voice cracking a little. She started sobbing again.

For some reason, that pulled the plug on my anger. I let her arm go and stepped back. It wasn't all that important a job, but it made Doris *feel* important. For a small town girl, that was a big deal. "I doubt the sheriff would fire you, not in this day and age."

"I don't think he'd wanna, but he'd have to."

"Why?" I was genuinely puzzled by her attitude toward the sheriff. Was the guy a bigot? Then again, a lot of people who were otherwise open-minded still had a thing about homosexuality.

"He'd have to, if he wanted to win re-election."

"Ah," I said, "and if he didn't fire you, the next sheriff would."

She nodded, sniffling softly.

I dug in my purse and found a little pack of tissues.

She looked surprised, then pulled out several and rubbed at the black mascara on her face. "Thanks."

I prompted her to return to her story. "So you and Julie were arguing, and Jimmy came home from his run…"

"We were in the bedroom. I don't know why I panicked. It's not like we were doing anything. I just had this crazy thought that he couldn't catch me in there. I realized later that he wouldn't have thought anything of it, if I'd played it cool." She fell silent, her gaze on the cement floor of the jail.

"Did Buddy bite you after you hit Jimmy?" I asked to get her rolling again. Eventually someone was going to come into the station, and I wanted the whole story before that happened.

She nodded her head. "Julie rushed out of the bedroom and grabbed the dog, tried to calm him down. She told me to just go, that she'd take care of things."

Doris raised her gaze to meet my eyes. Hers pooled with fresh tears. "So I did. And I never saw Julie alive again. I thought he had come to and they'd fought and he'd killed her. Honest, or I would've said something to the sheriff."

"Where'd the beer come from?"

Her mouth hung open for a second. "I don't know. I guess…"

"He swore he'd been sober for months, and there was no beer in the house. Did you smell beer on him?"

She tilted her head to one side. "No, come ta think of it, I didn't. At least not then."

"When did all this happen?"

"About eight to eight-fifteen was when Julie and me were talkin'."

I scrubbed a hand over my face. "And Jimmy was discovered about nine, right?"

She nodded, but her gaze flickered away from me. There was

something else she wasn't saying.

"Who was the caller? Who called in that they saw the door open?"

She shook her head, still not looking at me. "I, uh, didn't recognize the voice."

"Bull."

Her eyes darted back toward me, then her body sagged. "There was no caller. I tried Julie a couple a times on her cell and got no answer, so I went back to the house to check on her. I slipped around back and peeked into the kitchen. I could see down the hall to where Jimmy was sprawled out on the floor. I went in…"

She dropped her chin to her chest and her shoulders shook. "Julie was dead in the bedroom. I ran out the front door, didn't think to close it. Then I called the sheriff on the radio and said someone had called it in."

I wasn't sure I believed her. If her story was true, someone had less than a forty-five minute window to slip into the Garretts' house and kill Julie, then pour beer on Jimmy, all the while fending off the dog, and slip out again. All this without being seen or heard by Miss Shirley next door.

"Wait a minute," I said. "If Jimmy was out cold, how could he have killed Julie?"

She shrugged. "He did smell of beer then. I assumed he was drunk and had come to, hurt her, then passed out again."

"Was the vase there, on the floor, when you went back?"

She closed her eyes for a second, then opened them wide and shook her head. "No. There was flowers and water in it. They'd spilled all over the place. All that was gone when I went back. But Buddy was standin' over Jimmy, growlin' at me."

"Where was Ida Mae?"

"She was in her little pack-and-play. In the livin' room." Tears trickled again down Doris's cheeks. "She started cryin', durin' all the ruckus when I hit Jimmy and all. But when I went back in later, she was just sittin' in there, her thumb in her mouth." Her voice choked a little. "Her eyes were real big."

My throat ached. That poor child had witnessed whatever had happened to Jimmy. Thank God she hadn't been in the same room where her mother was murdered.

"You had coffee with Julie that morning?" I asked.

"Yes. We was sittin' in the kitchen. Then she went into the bedroom to get something and I followed her. That's when we started arguin'."

"I peeked in their kitchen window the other day. There were two mugs with lipstick stains in the drainer. So Julie had started to clean up…" I let my voice trail off, thinking she might volunteer something else.

But she just stared at me, her eyes hopeful. "Are ya gonna keep tryin' to figure out who killed her?" she finally asked, her voice plaintive. "I'll help all I can."

And in that moment, I believed her. I'd taken her by surprise and her confession seemed genuine. She wasn't the world's best liar. If she'd altered the story to cover her own part in Julie's death, I think I would have been able to tell something was off.

I opened my mouth to answer her question, even though I wasn't sure what I was going to say.

"Doris?" The sheriff's voice called out from the front of the station.

Her hand flew to her mouth. She held her face up to me. "Can ya tell I've been cryin'?"

"You've still got some mascara under your left eye."

She quickly licked her finger and rubbed under the eye.

"Got it."

She still didn't look great, but she'd probably pass for okay.

"Lemme go out first," she said. "I'll come get ya when he's in his office."

I agreed, since it would be hard to explain why we were having a girls' powwow in the cellblock. While she was gone, I tried to pull myself together. I was a bit rattled by the revelations I'd just heard.

After a few minutes, the door to the cell area opened and she gestured for me to come out. As I walked past her, she whispered, "Please don't tell him."

I didn't know what to say so I said nothing. I wasn't planning on repeating her confessions to Will Haines today, but in the future… I couldn't predict how things would pan out.

He greeted me at his office door with a smile. "To what do I owe this pleasant surprise?"

I stared at my empty hands. Somewhere along the way, I'd dropped the grilling fork. Doris appeared next to me and handed me the twisted piece of metal and plastic.

Surprisingly, Buddy didn't react to her presence. It was as if he knew she had come clean regarding her part in bringing about his owner's downfall.

I nodded a thank you to her as I took the fork. Then Buddy and I followed the sheriff into his office and I closed the door.

I placed the mangled clump of metal and plastic on his desk and took a deep breath. "Someone let an alligator into my house. That's what he did to the fork I used to stab a raw steak to lure him away from my dogs."

Will Haines blinked his baby blues a couple of times. "You wanna run that past me again."

"A gator was put in my living room while I was in the backyard working with the dogs. I think it was meant either to kill me, hurt me enough to put me out of commission, or scare me off from checking into Julie's death."

His mouth was hanging slightly open, his eyes wide, from either shock or disbelief. I was waiting for him to say I was overreacting, to assert that I'd left something open.

Instead he said, "You okay?"

I nodded.

"Were the dogs hurt?"

"No, just shook up."

He closed his mouth and narrowed his eyes at me. "Why are you still checking into Julie's death?"

"That's not the pertinent question here. Someone put a gator in my house!" My voice rose to a bit of a screech at the end.

"Did you leave a door or window open?"

I stifled a sigh. At least he hadn't said it as a statement, that I *must* have left something open. "No. The front door was locked. The back screen door was latched and within my sight. Someone picked the lock on the front and put the gator inside while we were out back."

"Did you call the county sheriff for your area?"

I deflated. It hadn't occurred to me to do so. "No."

"How do you know they picked the lock?"

"How else did they get in?"

"Were there scratch marks around the lock?"

"No." I *had* thought to check for that. "But can't someone pop a lock with a credit card?"

He shrugged. "It's not as easy as it sounds, but somebody who knows what they're doing could, or they used lock picks and were careful. You don't have deadbolts on your doors?"

"I do now, but I didn't when this happened."

"When did it happen?"

"Day before yesterday."

His eyebrows shot up. "And you're just now reporting it?" His tone was sharp.

I resisted the urge to hang my head. "I couldn't get down here before then."

"So again, why didn't you report it to your local sheriff?"

"And what would he have done?" I heard the defensiveness in my voice but couldn't seem to stop myself. "He'd have dismissed it. Told me I must've left a door open, and then he would have forgotten about it. But I always keep that front door locked, and the gator couldn't have gotten in the back without me noticing it."

Will Haines sat back in his desk chair. He waved a hand at me. "Would you sit down, please?"

I hadn't even realized I was still standing. I sank into the visitor's chair in front of the desk and signaled Buddy to lie down beside me.

The sheriff stared at the wall above my head for a few minutes. Finally he rubbed his chin. “So what have you found out while poking around?”

That brought me up short. And I had no clue what he already knew, or didn’t know. “Julie had an affair, while Jimmy was overseas.”

He nodded.

Okay, apparently he knew that.

“Somebody visited Julie that morning. The neighbor heard raised voices.”

“Could’ve been Julie and Jimmy.”

No, it couldn’t have been. Jimmy was still out cold when Doris came back and found Julie dead. But for some reason, I was reluctant to share Doris’s confession. If I believed she didn’t kill Julie, then why mess up her life unless it was necessary?

“Or it could’ve been Julie and somebody else.” Like Doris, or the killer. Most likely Doris. Suddenly I realized that I might be throwing the sheriff off the proper trail by focusing on the voices. “Miss Shirley also told me she saw flashes of tan through the bushes at times. She thinks it was someone’s clothing. Someone who was coming around back. Actually I think the word she used was *sneaking* around back.”

The sheriff sat up straighter in his chair. “That wasn’t in the report I got.”

“Humph.” I tried not to smirk. “She said she told it all to your deputy, Frank Larson.”

The sheriff’s mouth thinned into a grim line.

For a second, I fantasized what it would be like to kiss the frown lines around that mouth, to get him to relax those lips and… Warmth spread from my core right up into my face. I gave myself a good mental shake.

Fortunately, Will Haines was staring into space again. He tapped his lips with his fingertips. “Anything else?”

“There was no love lost between Julie and her brother.”

He let out a short bark of laughter. “That’s always been pretty obvious, ever since she and Jimmy moved back here."

A thought struck me. I had the urge to smack myself in the forehead. Why hadn't I looked into this angle sooner? "Who inherits Julie's share in the bank?"

"Held in trust for her daughter. Jimmy was the trustee. Back-up trustee is a lawyer in Lakeland. And I don't think Jimmy knew anything about that set-up. He was surprised when I told him he was the trustee, but not that the stocks went to the child. He said they'd discussed that."

"So you don't think he killed her to get control of the stocks. And John Collins wouldn't have control either. But did he know that?"

"No, I never thought Jimmy killed her over money. And John might not have control over her half, but he doesn't have her right under his nose anymore, questioning his decisions."

I raised my eyebrows in a tell-me-more expression.

He leaned forward. "Bank employees say there was a good bit of tension between them, but they get real vague when I ask for specifics."

"So he gets stuck with raising the kid, but he gets no control over her inheritance. Did he–"

The sheriff held up a hand. "He claims he did know about the trust, but I got no way of proving that one way or the other."

"Did the lawyer in Lakeland say whether or not he'd ever talked to John about it before Julie's death?"

"He says not, but John claims Julie told him herself. He does get a tidy monthly sum from the trust for the child's upkeep."

"How tidy a sum?" I asked.

"A thousand a month."

"Hmm. I don't see John Collins so hard up for money that he'd intentionally take on raising someone else's child for twelve grand a year."

"Yeah, and I doubt he'd risk murder just to get rid of a pesky sister," the sheriff said. "And Collins has an alibi. He went into work early that morning. Several bank employees vouched for that."

"Who's that leave?"

He shrugged, his shoulder muscles rippling under his uniform shirt. I averted my eyes.

"Nobody I can think of. Julie was well liked."

"But somebody's worried that I'm asking questions, else why the gator?"

"Yes, why indeed?" He pushed himself to a stand. "I'll contact the sheriff over your way and have him send a patrol car around to check your neighborhood regularly."

I stood as well. Buddy got up and gave himself a good shake.

I held out my hand. "Thanks for your time, Sheriff."

He grasped it, his palm dry and calloused. A tingling warmth spread up my arm. I quickly dropped his hand.

He smiled and handed me his card. "My cell number's on there. Don't hesitate to call if anything else happens." Then his expression sobered. "And be careful who you talk to about all this. As far as we know, anyone in this town could be a killer."

The words barely registered. I'd noticed for the first time that he had dimples when he smiled.

"And please, *stop* investigating, Marcia," he said, his voice more firm now. "I *am* continuing to look into the case."

I nodded, unable to think coherently, my eyes glued once again to the corner of his mouth, where that dimple had been a few seconds ago.

He sketched me a small salute as I backed toward the door, my dog following along. Buddy looked over his shoulder and wagged his tail, his own canine salute to the sheriff.

The sexy hunk of a sheriff.

I was breathing heavy by the time I got to my car, and it had nothing to do with the heat. Not the outside temperature, at least. My internal temperature was another thing all together.

Something had melted inside when he'd said my first name, *and* pronounced it correctly.

CHAPTER SIXTEEN

I woke up in the dark with the creepy feeling that I was being watched. I turned on the light. Buddy stood next to my bed, staring at me. He woofed softly and wagged his tail.

"What's up?" I mumbled. "You need to go out? It's the middle of the night."

By way of an answer, he lay down on the small rug beside the bed. Guess not.

I rolled over and tried to go back to sleep, but I couldn't shake the creepy feeling. I got up and put on my robe. Maybe some chamomile tea would help.

As I walked through the shadowy living room, Buddy on my heels, I veered toward the front door to check the deadbolt and the alarm. Then I shifted the curtain of the front window aside and stared out at the street.

I realized with a jolt that it wasn't empty. A Collinsville Sheriff's Department patrol car was parked at the curb, the silhouette of a head in the driver's seat.

I grabbed my purse from the sofa and dug out my cell phone and the sheriff's card.

One ring. "Haines."

The quick response added to my suspicions. "What are you doing out there?"

"The local sheriff couldn't spare anybody. Said he had a meth lab raid happening tonight. So I thought I'd keep an eye on things myself."

Before some saner part of me had time to protest I found myself saying, “Get in here.”

I turned off the alarm and opened the front door.

Lacy was asleep in her crate. She roused at the sound of the sheriff’s deep voice.

“It’s okay, girl,” I said. “Go back to sleep.”

Will Haines started to hold out his hand for Buddy to sniff, then stopped with it halfway there.

“It’s okay when he’s not working,” I said.

He lowered the hand. Buddy looked at me and I nodded. He sniffed the extended fingers, then licked them.

I chuckled. “You have now received the official seal of approval.”

The sheriff smiled, flashing white teeth and dimples. “Glad I pass muster.”

I ducked my head and turned quickly to lead the way into the kitchen. “He’s a bit on the picky side,” I said over my shoulder, “so feel free to be impressed with yourself.”

I gestured toward the table while heading for the counter to put on some coffee.

He raised an eyebrow at the sight of the word *decaf* on the bag of beans. “Make mine caffeinated. I need to stay awake.”

“No, you don’t. You can sleep on my couch. I think two dogs, an alarm, and a cop car outside should be sufficient deterrent.”

“You didn’t tell me you got an alarm.”

I pointed out the little magnets on the back door. He burst out laughing.

“Hey, it’s pretty darn loud. I’d demonstrate but it would set the dogs off.”

He held up his hands in a surrender gesture. “Okay, I’ll stop making fun of your alarm system.”

I grinned in spite of myself. “Not sure I’d call it a *system*.”

When the coffee finished gurgling into the pot, I brought it and two mugs to the table and asked about cream and sugar. He declined both.

We sat and drank coffee in companionable silence for a few minutes. Then we both started talking at once.

"How long have you been down…"

"Why didn't you send one of your men…"

We both stopped, chuckled nervously. Suddenly I felt like a teenager on a first date. I ground my teeth quietly. "You were about to say?"

He waved his hand in a casual gesture, a soft smile on his face. "Ladies first."

I tried not to let his dimples distract me. "I was about to ask why you didn't send one of your men here. Isn't guarding someone a bit beneath the sheriff himself?"

He shifted one shoulder in a half shrug. "Can't send my men outside of my jurisdiction. Officially, I'm off duty right now."

Did that mean he was taking a special interest in me, or was he just indulging an overactive sense of duty? Perhaps amplified by his guilt over Jimmy's suicide.

"I was about to ask how long you've lived in Florida," he said.

We shared a little about our backgrounds while we finished our coffee. I told him about growing up in the suburbs of Baltimore, with my Episcopal rector father, now deceased, and my mother, the nurse.

"You've heard the one about the little kid with that background, haven't you?" I asked.

He shook his head.

"She was overheard one day muttering to herself, 'Jesus and germs, Jesus and germs, that's all I ever hear around here, and I haven't seen either one yet.'"

It was an old joke but he chuckled appreciatively. "How'd you end up down here?" he asked.

Which led to the tale of how I met and married Ted, the philandering violinist, and the rapid decline of our ill-fated marriage–which took all of five minutes to tell, that's how short and boring that marriage was.

The sheriff looked grim when I mentioned Ted's cheating.

"I'd never liked the cold winters," I said, "so I decided to move down here for a fresh start. How about you? Ever been married?"

He took a sip of coffee. "For three years." Then he asked me another question.

I hadn't talked so much about myself in ages. The man was a good listener. But he got cagey whenever things got too specific on his end.

He had secrets, and secrets meant baggage.

I don't need that, I told myself.

He flashed his dimples at me and certain parts of myself stopped listening to that sage inner voice. It was getting hot in the room.

I considered getting up to turn on the ceiling fan, but was suddenly self-conscious in my old chenille robe. I couldn't remember the last time I'd thrown it in the washer while doing laundry.

"That pink's a good color on you." He gestured toward the robe. "Brings out the red in your hair."

My hand flew to my hair, which I hadn't bothered to comb. It was probably sticking out in all directions.

Wait a minute! How'd he know I was thinking about my robe? I narrowed my eyes at him.

He looked pointedly at my other hand, which was clutching the lapels of the robe collar closed at my neck.

Crapola. He can read me like a book.

I'd have to rein myself in better. The man was a trained investigator after all–he'd told me he was a homicide detective on the Albany police force in New York State before moving south.

I raised the coffee pot in the air, being the polite hostess offering more coffee, but secretly praying he'd say no. I was back to feeling like a self-conscious teenager, and I hated that feeling.

He did decline the offer, then pushed himself to a stand. "Where's the couch?"

I jumped up. "I'll get you some sheets." I went to the linen closet and rummaged for a matching set. Then made a quick detour to the bathroom mirror to check on my hair. It wasn't too bad so I let it be. If I combed it now, the sheriff might read something into that.

When I got back to the living room, he was standing by the door, his cowboy hat in his hand.

"I'm thinking I'd better sleep in the car after all."

I clutched the sheets against my chest and stepped toward him. "Why?"

He reached out and tipped my chin up. His lips brushed mine. They were warm and soft and his breath smelled of coffee, with a hint of mint.

He pulled his head back and smiled. "That's why."

My knees went all wobbly at the sight of those dimples.

He grinned and wrapped an arm around my back. He kissed me again, deeper this time.

My brain froze and my rebellious body took over. It melted against him, the forgotten sheets sliding to the floor. Delicious tingling sparked down my core.

He let go of me and went out the door.

I sucked in air and caught the remnants of his woodsy aftershave wafting back toward me. I watched his tight buns, clad in snug jeans rather than his uniform slacks, as he sauntered down my front walk, his hat on his head at a jaunty angle.

His confidence both attracted and grated. Pretty darn cocky of him to think he could just kiss me like that.

Then he turned and sketched a salute before climbing into his car. "Thanks for the coffee," he called out softly.

I found myself giving him a simpering smile and a little wave. My inner voice suggested that I slap myself silly.

I opted against the self-abuse and took myself back to bed.

The cruiser was gone when I got up the next morning. I considered calling Will Haines and thanking him for keeping watch over me. But I decided that could be misinterpreted as my being interested in him.

Well, yeah!

"Whose side are you on?" I said out loud to my inner voice.

It kept its own counsel.

I slurped coffee–high test this time–at the kitchen table and tried to decide what to do about the Garrett case. Should I butt out?

I admitted to myself that I didn't have much choice. I was fresh out of leads. I had no clue who had entered the Garrett house during that precious forty-five minutes and had taken advantage of the fact that Jimmy was out cold on the floor, a perfect patsy for Julie's murder.

But my eyes stung at the thought of Jimmy's suicide. Why had he given up so quickly?

I rubbed my eyes and rooted in my robe pocket for a tissue. Easy for me to say. I hadn't been the one locked up in a cage, believing the whole town was against me. And he'd already been struggling with the residuals of PTSD, plus the grief of losing his wife. Who was I to judge him for giving up?

I gave into the urge and put my head down on my crossed arms on the table to have a good cry. A few minutes later, a cold nose nudged my arm.

When I looked up, Buddy tilted his head, as if to say, *Why are you crying? You've got me.*

Guilt made me cry harder, because I was secretly glad to have Buddy back in my life permanently. Then my stomach clenched. Technically, Buddy belonged to Jimmy's estate. Would John Collins try to take him away from me?

Yet another good reason to stay away from Collinsville, Florida.

I pulled myself together and headed for my bedroom. As I got dressed, I realized I felt better. My good cry had been cathartic. Maybe I'd cancel that appointment with the counselor for next Monday.

Or maybe you still need it. Again, my inner voice sounded suspiciously like my mother.

The mail carrier beeped her horn, as she did every morning,

to let me and my neighbor know that she had delivered earth-shatteringly important missives to our mailboxes.

I dutifully shuffled out to my mailbox. I paused and took a deep breath of warm air. Yup, spring had arrived in Mayfair. Across from my house, wild flowers bloomed amongst the palmetto fronds along the edge of the road. I glanced down the street toward the motel, then shielded my eyes from the morning sun. Sure enough, there was a sprinkling of rosy red on Edna's azalea bushes, which rose as high as the first floor of the building. Florida azaleas were different from those up north–they grew taller with bigger leaves and heartier blooms. And those blooms burst forth at the first sign of warmer weather.

I smiled and grabbed my mail out of the box.

I was rifling through the junk mail, looking for those all-important missives, when I ran into my next-door neighbor, literally. I jumped back a step.

Today Sherie Wells wore a dark green shirtwaist dress that had gone out of style decades ago. Her silver-streaked black hair was pulled back in a chignon. She looked every inch the schoolteacher she had once been, a schoolteacher with very little tolerance for misbehaving children.

She raised one eyebrow and bore into my skull with her chocolate-brown eyes. "You had some emergency last night, I suppose?"

That was Southern for "What the heck was a police officer doing at your house in the middle of the night?"

"Uh, no ma'am," I stammered. "I, uh… Sheriff Haines is a…" Was he a friend? I guess I could claim him as such after that kiss last night. "He's a friend, and he happened to be in the area, uh, on police business, so he stopped by for a cup of coffee."

Mrs. Wells shifted eyebrows, her body language quite eloquently saying, *at three in the morning?*

I wanted to shrink into the sidewalk but I forced myself to stand up straight, holding my junk mail against my chest like a shield. "Decaf," I said, a touch of defiance in my voice.

Mercifully, Edna Mayfair came along, walking her dogs. Today's muumuu sported tropical flowers in a hideous shade of yellow that I hoped never to encounter in nature. Over it she wore a brown man's sweater–probably Dexter's, although it was moth-eaten enough it could have once belonged to her brother, old man Mayfair. It hung loosely from her rounded shoulders.

Her dogs hurried over to sniff at my tennis shoes.

Edna tugged gently on their leashes. "Behave, you two."

They ignored her and jumped up on my jeans-clad leg to beg for an ear scratch. I obliged.

"Mornin', Sherie." Edna nodded her head toward me in greeting. "Marcia. Looks like it's gonna be a gorgeous day."

Mrs. Wells was not to be deterred. "Marcia had a visitor last night." She paused for effect. "In the middle of the night. Some sheriff *friend*."

"Oh yeah?" Edna said, most unhelpfully.

"He was just checking on me, making sure I was *all right*." I came down hard on the last two words and stared pointedly at Edna, hoping she'd get the connection to the gator invasion. I'd asked her and Dexter to keep the whole incident to themselves. Miraculously, no one had been out and about when Dexter had hauled the dazed reptile out of my backyard. (I'd found out the next day that Mrs. Wells had been away, helping her daughter-in-law with a new baby.)

Edna was normally good at keeping people's confidences, but I wasn't at all sure she wouldn't buckle under Mrs. Wells' unrelenting gaze.

Edna turned slightly and gave me a quick wink, making me ashamed of my lack of faith. "I heard on the news this mornin' that the sheriff, our sheriff that is, busted some druggies last night that were runnin' a meth lab up toward Ocala. I'll bet Marcia's friend was helpin' out with that raid."

I flashed her a grateful smile.

"Humph," Mrs. Wells said, her nose tilted upward. "And he thought three in the mornin' was a respectable time to drop by?"

Edna smiled. "Aw, Sherie, they're young. They don't need their sleep like us old folks."

Once again I marveled at how whites and blacks interacted in Florida. I assumed it came from generations of blacks living in white households–cooking and keeping house and raising their children–interacting daily despite the differences in their social standing. Definitely, bigotry was still alive and well on a deeper level, but most of the time on the surface there was an ease between the races that was subtly different from the stiff distance, and sometimes simmering antagonism, in the north.

"Harumph," Mrs. Wells said. Then she turned to me and her expression softened. "You just make sure that young man doesn't take advantage of you."

I was totally flummoxed. Warmth spread through my chest, then rose to my cheeks. "Uh, I won't. Thanks…thank you, ma'am, for…" I stuttered to a halt, took a deep breath. "I'm truly touched by your concern, ma'am. I won't let him take advantage." Then I quickly added, "Not that I think he intends to."

Mrs. Wells smiled at Edna, and then she shocked me again by patting my arm. "Y'all have a good day."

I restrained myself until I got back inside my house. Then I shook my head and laughed out loud. Apparently I had been adopted as part of the Wells' clan.

While driving to Ocala for a training session with Pete and Max, something was niggling at the back of my brain. It wasn't until later that afternoon, as I was heading home, that it finally floated to the surface.

The tiny piece of beige cloth caught in Buddy's collar.

It was probably from Doris's sleeve, from when Buddy bit her.

But what if it wasn't?

Driving one-handed–my car was born before Bluetooth–I dug my cell phone out of my purse and called the Collinsville Sheriff's Department. Doris answered and I asked without preamble, "Did Buddy tear your shirt that morning, when he bit you?"

Silence, except for the distant rumble of that ancient air compressor. "No, I had my sleeves rolled up at Julie's house. I rolled them down later, to hide the bite marks."

"You don't have a little tear in that shirt?" I asked, double-checking.

"No. Why?"

For some reason, I was reluctant to tell her. She'd offered to help investigate, but I didn't trust her completely. I ignored her question and asked another of my own. "You said Julie had been preoccupied. Any other thoughts on what that was about?"

More air-conditioner rumbling. "One time, when I asked her what was bothering her, she said she didn't want to stir up trouble until she was sure."

"So whatever she was checking out would cause trouble for someone." And possibly give that someone a motive for murder. But who and what was Julie checking out?

"Something at the bank?"

"Maybe," Doris said. "But Julie'd got herself elected to the town council a few months ago. She said they were a contentious bunch sometimes. I wondered if what was botherin' her had to do with them. One time she said somethin' about them needin' to clean up their act."

Since I was driving, I started a mental list, with *town council* as the first entry.

"What about John Collins' admin assistant at the bank?" Had she been giving me the evil eye that day just because she recognized me and couldn't wait to tell her boss on me, or did she have something else to hide?

"Carol Reynolds? She's a newcomer. Been at the bank 'bout four years, but she don't live here no more. She moved down to Polk City 'bout a year ago."

I shook my head at the small town concept of newcomer. I was grateful that the long-term residents of Mayfair weren't as insular as those in Collinsville seemed to be. Then again, my neighbors had been so desperate to see their almost ghost town revived, they probably would've welcomed the devil if he'd moved in next door.

I added *Carol Reynolds* to my mental list. Then still fishing for fresh leads, I said, "How about John Collins? You said he had friends in Orlando, but is there anybody locally he's close to?"

"His ole buddies from high school, Frank Larson and Dwayne Snyder."

The first of those names took me by surprise. "As in Deputy Frank?"

"Yeah," Doris said. "They were on the football team together. John was the quarterback. The girls were all over him back then."

"You don't like Collins, do you?"

"Not particularly, no." She didn't elaborate but I could guess her reasons. I didn't particularly like him either.

I thanked her and disconnected.

As soon as I got home and had let the dogs out for a bathroom break, I fired up my laptop.

A half hour later, I had zip on Carol Reynolds except a possible address in Polk City. Apparently she had led a very uneventful life. I had even less for Frank Larson and Dwayne Snyder. The latter had no online presence at all and the only mentions of Frank were related to his position in the sheriff's department.

The website for the town of Collinsville mentioned the town council, its duties and how often it met, etc., but it didn't list the members. If I wanted to pursue that angle, I'd have to get their names from Doris.

That led me back to the scrap of cloth. Had Doris been lying? Her encounter with Buddy, while Jimmy lay there unconscious, could have been worse than she'd described. Especially if she'd already killed Julie, who therefore couldn't have intervened as she'd claimed.

But if Doris was telling the truth, then someone else had a close encounter with Buddy. Was it the guy who'd tranquilized him, to get him to let them approach Jimmy? Or was it someone trying to pour beer on Jimmy? Julie's murderer?

Okay, I needed to get a grip. I wasn't supposed to be investigating anymore, and if I kept this up I would blow my chances with the hunky sheriff.

I called his cell phone. I wasn't sure whether I was relieved or disappointed when I got his voicemail. Maybe some of both. I left a message. "Can't remember if I told you that Julie had been preoccupied lately. Could be about the town council or something going on at the bank. Oh, and there's that tan piece of cloth I found in Buddy's collar. Uh..." I couldn't think of anything else to say so I disconnected.

There. I'd turned it over to the sheriff.

He called back a half hour later.

I stared at his name on my caller ID screen for a couple of seconds before answering. "Hello."

"Hey Marcia, what's with the cryptic message?"

"Uh." I swallowed. "I'd forgotten about that piece of cloth I found, you know, in Buddy's collar. So I, um, thought you might have too. Forgotten it, I mean."

And you wanted an excuse to call him, my inner voice piped up.

"Ah, shut up," I muttered under my breath.

"What?"

"Oh, uh, bad connection." I made some noises that I hoped sounded like static on the line.

"And no, you hadn't told me about Julie being preoccupied. Who told you that?"

"Doris."

"You two have gotten real chummy lately."

I snorted under my breath. I was pretty sure Doris was only tolerating me–one, because I knew her secret and two, because she wanted me to find out who killed Julie. Or at least that's what she said.

"Say, are you busy this evening?" His voice had dropped, as if maybe he didn't want anyone else to hear him. "I thought I might take you to dinner, you know, before I set up housekeeping out front at the curb."

My heart raced–one part excitement, one part panic. My head scrambled for something to say. "I'm not dealing well with this… this letting-the-investigation-go thing." Okay, those were *not* the most ideal words for the situation.

Silence. I counted the seconds ticking by. *One-one thousand, two-one thousand, three-one thousand, four…*

"I noticed. But it wasn't your investigation to begin with." The tone was carefully controlled. He was pissed.

"Yeah, I know, but at first I didn't think you were investigating. I mean it seemed like you thought Jimmy had done it and the case was closed."

Another beat of silence. "But now you know that I am investigating."

"Yeah." I paused, then asked, "Who do you suspect?" My voice sounded more tentative than I would have preferred.

"I can't discuss that with civilians."

Ouch!

"John Collins?" I said. He didn't have much of a motive but he seemed to dislike Julie.

Then again, lots of siblings weren't crazy about each other on the surface but loved each other deep down. My own brother and I weren't super close. He might conceivably grab my arm and maybe even shake me a little if we were in a really bad argument, but I couldn't imagine him hitting me, much less banging my head on a radiator.

The sound of air being blown out. "You're forgetting Collins has an alibi for that morning."

For a second, I fantasized about the sheriff blowing air into my ear in person–warm, moist air. My nether regions perked up.

I shook my head to clear it, then wracked my brain for something else to ask him. Who could he possibly be investigating?

My head swam. I'd lost my bearings. My focus for the last couple of weeks had been on proving Jimmy's innocence. But now I knew that Will Haines also believed he was innocent, and he was investigating.

So suddenly I was supposed to back off? Just go back to my regular routine as if nothing had happened to the Garretts?

"I'm sorry, Sheriff. I…" I trailed off, not sure what exactly I was sorry for, but still pretty sure I owed the man an apology.

"It's okay, Marcia." His tone was softer. "You cared about the Garretts. I… That's an admirable trait."

"Uh, about this evening. I hate to be such a bother. You don't need to drive all the way up here and camp out at my curb. Surely the local sheriff's department can send somebody around now. They can't be raiding meth labs two nights in a row."

Was that a sigh I detected?

"They're still pretty busy, but you should be okay."

Disappointment clogged my throat. He'd given up awfully easily. A part of me wanted to say, "We could meet for dinner somewhere anyway." But I couldn't get it out. Fear of rejection is a powerful thing. Or maybe I was more afraid that he would agree.

He was still talking. "…gator was probably meant to be a warning, so as long as you're not poking around down here, I doubt anything else will happen."

"Thank you, Sheriff, for being so… concerned. And, uh, thanks for the dinner invitation."

He cleared his throat. "Maybe some other time. In the meantime, do me a favor, would you?"

"What's that?"

"Call me Will."

Butterflies danced in my stomach. I was perfectly fine with him calling me Marcia. So why so resistant to calling him Will?

"Sure… uh, Will." It sounded totally awkward to my ears, but he seemed to accept it.

We exchanged goodbyes and I disconnected, then blew out air. "Ho, boy."

CHAPTER SEVENTEEN

The next morning, I was restless and cranky. I went to Ocala and spent two hours with Pete and Max. Pete was doing beautifully now. He and Max were truly becoming partners. We scheduled our next training session for Sunday afternoon.

I left Pete's place and the restless, cranky mood immediately returned.

There was no more murder investigation to add excitement to my life. And I was pretty sure I'd dashed cold water all over Will Haines' interest in me by turning down his dinner invitation.

Even Lacy was beyond the challenging phase in her training now. She caught on to new skills quickly and was firming up her responses to previously taught signals.

Time to readjust to boring normalcy.

At home, I sat down at my kitchen table with a peanut butter and banana sandwich, one of my go-to comfort foods. My phone pinged in my jeans' pocket. Ignoring the tiny frisson of excitement–maybe it was the hunky sheriff–I wiggled my butt around to fish the phone out.

A text from Becky. *Haven't heard from u in a while. What's going on?*

I also ignored my disappointment as I called her.

"Sorry, Beck," I said into the phone when she answered. "Life's been a bit crazy lately." I hadn't talked to her since the afternoon of the gator invasion, so I filled her in on recent events.

"What makes you so sure that you've blown it with *Will*?" She emphasized his name, making me wish I hadn't told her about his request to call him that.

"I'm not sure, but he was pretty pissed about my butting into his investigation. And he didn't push it about the dinner invite."

"Sounds to me like you blew him off, so of course he didn't push it. Man's got his ego to protect."

"Lord save me from male egos."

"Yeah, but the bodies that come attached to some of those egos are often worth the price of admission."

I visualized Will Haines' buff body, clad in his snug jeans and crisp uniform shirt, and felt my face flush.

"So do you like this guy or not?" Becky asked.

"Yes, no. I don't know." The warmth in my cheeks descended down through my chest to my nether regions. They cast their vote in the "yes" column.

A snort and a snicker came from the phone. "That's my girl. Always knows her own mind."

Becky and I chatted for a few more minutes. Then as we were signing off, I remembered a favor I wanted to ask of her. "Can you come over later? I could use your help with a training session with Lacy."

"Yeah, I'll be finished with clients by two, could be there by three. What do you need me to do?"

"Be a passerby."

"Huh?"

"I'll explain when you get here."

Truth was I didn't have all the details worked out myself. Lacy was the first dog I was training for a female veteran. Rainey Bryant was an army nurse who had been sexually assaulted by a fellow soldier during her second deployment in Afghanistan. She had issues that went beyond those normally obtained from being in a combat zone for a few too many months.

When I'd gone to her house to introduce her to Lacy, Rainey had confided that one of her greatest fears was that she would be raped again. She'd wanted me to train Lacy to attack if someone was hurting her. I'd pointed out that neither collies nor Alaskan huskies were particularly protective breeds. Did she want me to get her a different dog, a German shepherd perhaps? No, she'd replied, she really liked Lacy.

I'd gotten Rainey's permission to talk to her counselor, who had confirmed that she was downright obsessed about being assaulted again.

The maneuver I was going to try to teach Lacy I had dubbed the Lassie response. Since the service dogs had to interact with people on a regular basis–both the owner's family and strangers–they had to tamp down some of their natural territorial tendencies, which was incompatible with the role of guard dog. But I was hoping that I might be able to train a dog to get help.

We'd see if it worked or not. I suspected it would be a *not*, but it was worth a try.

The signal I'd decided on was "Run," combined with a shooing motion with my hand. It couldn't be anything more explicit, or the attacker might realize the dog was going for help and would try to stop the animal.

If Lieutenant Bryant did encounter a rapist again, Lacy might or might not be able to find someone to come to her aid in time to do much good. But knowing that the dog was trained to go for help might give my client more confidence in her day-to-day life.

I was discovering that trauma not only caused nightmares and flashbacks that jolted the person back to the scary past, but it also stole their peace of mind about the present and the future as well.

I'd already worked with Lacy several times on the first step, and by the time Becky arrived later that afternoon, the dog was consistently running to the gate when I gave the signal. Later, I would teach her to respond to *either* the verbal or the hand gesture, but for now I used them together.

Buddy had watched our performance from his favorite spot under the magnolia tree, raising his big black head occasionally and tilting it. If that dog could talk, I figured he'd be saying, "What the heck are you doing?"

"I wish I knew, boy." I leaned down to give him a pat.

I explained to Becky what I wanted her to do, then waited as she crossed the backyard and went out the gate, leaving it open behind her. Lacy always came now when I called her name, so I wasn't concerned that she would run off.

At the other end of the yard, I gave Lacy the hand signal. "Run, girl!"

She took off for the gate but came to a screeching halt when she got there. She looked back over her shoulder at me.

I made the shooing motion again. "Run, Lacy, run!"

She stood frozen, staring at me. Then I heard Becky's voice calling to her from the street. "Come here, girl."

Lacy pranced through the gate, her fluffy white tail wagging tentatively.

For this second step in the process, Becky would lead Lacy back to me. I heard her say, "Hey there, sweetie. Where's your owner?"

Then things went awry. Buddy jumped up and raced after Lacy.

Shaking my head, I jogged after him, wondering if using him as a mentor had him now thinking he was Lacy's keeper. When I reached the gate I was greeted by the sight of Buddy herding Lacy back toward the backyard and Becky looking flustered.

I blew out air. "Thanks, Becky."

"You gonna try again."

"Yeah, that's how this works. Repetition until you're sick of it." I led the way back through the gate, Lacy and Buddy trailing behind. Becky stayed out by the street.

I pointed to the magnolia tree. "Buddy, lie down."

He gave me an inscrutable look and did as he'd been told.

I went through the whole "Run" routine again. Lacy's hesitation at the gate was shorter this time.

Becky and I worked with her for another hour, with Buddy looking on. Lacy loved this new game, but I wasn't at all sure how to convey the next step to her. The idea was to get her to bark persistently and then run away a bit, then look back and bark again, trying to get the passerby to follow her.

I waved Becky into the backyard. “That’s enough for today.”

“That’s it?” she said, wiping sweat from her forehead with the back of her hand.

“For now. We’ll reinforce this much when you can spare some time again. Then I need to figure out how to break down the rest of it into smaller steps. Maybe I’ll call Mattie and see if anybody’s done this before.” And while I was at it, I could ask her about protocols for training mentor dogs.

“Good idea,” Becky said. “Now, gimme some sweet tea before I pass out.”

I crated Lacy and gave Buddy the off-duty signal. Then Becky and I settled around the kitchen table with a pitcher of tea and two glasses. I nudged the sugar bowl in her direction.

She scrunched up her nose. “You know it’s not the same when you don’t brew it with the sugar in it.”

“Yeah, but since I haven’t figured out a way to extract sugar from it later…” I intentionally trailed off and took a big swig of my barely sweetened tea.

Buddy came into the kitchen and made a beeline for Becky. He plopped his big head into her lap and she scratched behind his ears.

My phone buzzed in my pocket. I pulled it out and stared at the caller ID.

“Who is it?” Becky said.

“Sheriff Hunky.”

I swallowed hard and answered the call. “Hi, Sheriff… uh, Will.”

“Hey Marcia, I was wondering if I could cash in that rain check for dinner tonight.”

I glanced at the clock. It was already five. “Uh, it’s kinda late.”

“I’m actually on the road. I had to come up toward your way to talk to somebody. I thought I could swing on by.”

I couldn’t think of what to say. Was I just a convenient stop off when he was already in the area? Or was he using that as a way to keep it casual? I couldn't blame him. That way, he would be able to save face if I said no.

"Uh, we could go to Belleview, I guess. There's a decent Italian place there."

"Yeah, that'd be okay. But there's a new place opened up on 301, a little ways south of there. It's French cuisine, but not fancy or anything. I've heard the food is good."

"Well, I've got company at the moment."

"Oh?" His voice sounded funny.

"I was just leaving," Becky said in a loud voice.

"Your friend could come with us," the sheriff said, his voice now an odd mixture of relieved and reluctant.

Becky was shaking her head vigorously.

"No," I said. "I think she has to get back to Ocala. Maybe another time. She can join us, I mean… another time." I was blabbering but couldn't seem to stop myself. "I mean, we can go, just the two of us this time."

A rush of air being expelled on the other end of the line. "That sounds fine. When shall I pick you up?"

"Why don't I meet you there, say around six-thirty. We've been working with one of the dogs so I need a shower."

"Sounds good." He gave me the address. "Like I said, it's not fancy. Jeans are fine."

"Okay, see ya there." I glanced at Becky as I disconnected. Her face was beet red. "What the…?"

Suddenly she let out her pent-up breath with a loud "Woot!" She jumped up and did a jig around the kitchen. "Marcia's got a da-ate! Marcia's got a da-ate!"

Buddy looked at her and tilted his head.

"Sheez, Beck, you don't have to sound so surprised."

"And when was the last time you had a date?"

I grimaced. I hadn't since I'd known her, not since coming to Florida. My last date had been a disastrous blind set-up by a friend back in Maryland shortly after my divorce. I shuddered at the memory. Reminders of that night were not the best thing for my confidence right now. Thankfully I didn't have too much time to think about it all.

Becky fed and watered the dogs for me while I showered. Then we both stood in front of my closet as I agonized over what to wear.

Will Haines had emphasized casual, so it was a safe bet he would be wearing jeans. But should I wear blue jeans or the dressier black pair? And what about a top? Should I wear…

Becky pulled my favorite turquoise blouse off the hanger and thrust it at me. "Put it on, for Pete's sake. You know it's what you'll feel most comfortable in."

I gave her a grateful smile. Comfort would have no place in her own choice of wardrobe for a date, but she knew me well. I would be squirmy and irritable in anything that was too tight, too short or too glitzy.

Finally I was dressed, hair brushed up into a shiny ponytail and a touch of makeup to bolster my ego. Once in my car, I almost got cold feet, but Becky smiling and waving from my own front porch inspired me to turn on the ignition and pull away from the curb.

Will Haines was waiting in front of the entrance to the small restaurant, which was called simply *Pierre's*. He was wearing jeans, with a short-sleeved, chambray shirt that brought out the blue of his eyes, a denim jacket slung over one shoulder. His hair was neatly combed and looked a bit damp. It could have been from perspiration–the day had been warmer than usual for this time of year–but as I got closer I caught a whiff of soap.

So his claim that he was already in the area was a white lie.

I was okay with that. It made me feel warm inside that he had gone to some lengths to contrive an opportunity to see me.

He broke into a smile as I approached. Then there was an awkward moment while he seemed to try to decide if he should kiss my cheek, shake my hand or take my elbow. He finally stepped back and made an after-you gesture.

We were seated by Pierre himself in a dim room that smelled delicious. My stomach gurgled loudly. I breathed deeply of the medley of aromas.

The sheriff ordered something with *boeuf* in it, and I pointed to the word *poulet* on the menu. I was pretty sure that was chicken.

"Excellent choice, *madame*." Pierre beamed at me.

The conversation was awkward at first, but by the time I'd downed half a glass of the white wine Will had ordered, he and I were chatting away. The tension in my shoulders eased some. I might just survive this evening.

He dropped several hints about age differences and it finally dawned on me that he was fishing for my age. "I'm thirty-two," I said.

"Really?"

I preened a little, assuming he'd thought I was younger than that.

He sat back in his chair. "I'm thirty-eight."

I swallowed quickly to stifle my own *Really?* that had almost escaped my lips. I'd thought him older than that.

Six years, I thought. *Not too big a gap for a couple.*

I shuddered slightly. That word *couple* scared the crap out of me.

"I'm relieved," Will said.

The comment had me shaking my head in confusion.

"I thought you might be older than me."

"What?" I exclaimed, shooting daggers at him with my eyes.

Will quickly held up his hand, palm out. "No, no. That didn't come out right. You don't look older. But you don't always sound like a normal Millennial."

My stomach churned. Wine without food maybe wasn't a great idea when your date turned out to be a jerk. My chest ached with an old pain.

I blinked hard. "I think I'm pretty normal," I said carefully.

Will leaned forward and grabbed one of my hands. I tried to pull away, but he grasped it tight between both of his.

"I'm sorry. I hit a nerve, didn't I?"

I shook my head vehemently. "It's just that I've struggled all my life to be normal."

"Why?" Will's expression said he was genuinely perplexed.

"I don't know." I flashed back to middle school–the purgatory of the Earth plane–and the boys following me down the hall chanting "Mar-SEE-a, Mar-SEE-a."

"I, uh, got teased a lot as a kid, because of my name."

"So why didn't you change it?"

I shrugged, suddenly feeling like that thirteen-year-old middle schooler again.

"Bill was my nickname as a kid," he said, "but I never liked it. When I moved down here, I started going by Will."

I gave him a weak smile. "I like Will better."

"Me, too. It's more distinctive."

I tried harder for a true smile, the tightness in my chest loosening some. "Uh, what did you mean about me not sounding like a Millennial?"

It was his turn to shrug. "I don't know. I guess because you sound more mature than that. The words that you use sometimes, they sound older."

I let out a self-conscious laugh. "Thank you, Mom! Remember my father was an Episcopal priest. She drummed into my brother and me that we had to behave, not curse, et cetera. In self-defense, I took on some of her speech patterns."

Will smiled. "Okay, yeah, that explains a lot."

The entrees arrived, and he let go of my hand to top off our wineglasses. Cognizant of the fact that I had to drive myself home, I sipped sparingly. The chicken thingie I'd ordered was delicious and I tried not to wolf it down.

I caught Will smiling indulgently as I shoveled another bite into my mouth. I rolled my eyes to show that it was so good I couldn't resist gobbling. His grin broadened.

He started up the conversation again. "I kinda miss having you stop by the department."

"Well, you wanted me to butt out, didn't you?"

"Yeah. But I still miss seeing that flash of red hair going past my office door."

I started to return his smile, then remembered the reason I was no longer visiting the Collinsville Sheriff's Department regularly. My mood sobered considerably.

He grimaced. "Sorry. Hey, are you a University of Florida fan?"

I appreciated his sensitivity to the shift in my mood, but the change of subject was rather abrupt. "Uh, I'm not much on football, but I follow the Gators' basketball team."

"Great. I've got a chance to get a couple of tickets to a game this Saturday. But I wasn't sure it was worth it to drive up there to go by myself. You wanna come?"

Again, a bit of equivocating to save his ego if I said no. Or had he caught on that I was skittish and he was trying not to scare me off?

"That's a long drive," I stalled. "What time's the game?"

"Three in the afternoon, so it won't be too late finishing up."

"Yeah, but it would be close to midnight by the time you got home. That's a lot of driving in one day."

Will shook his head slightly. "I figured I'd stay at the Mayfair Motel and drive home Sunday morning. I usually stay in Gainesville with the friend that I'm getting the tickets from. But he's traveling on business this weekend."

I stalled some more by taking a sip of wine. His expression was carefully neutral but he was cutting his meat into ridiculously tiny pieces. Finally he forked one of the pieces into his mouth.

Why was I torturing the man? Most of me wanted to say yes, but the part of me that was screaming no was a nervous wreck.

He chewed and swallowed. "So you wanna go?"

"I guess. I mean, sure. Sounds like fun."

He pointed his fork at me. "You know, Marcia Banks, you could give a man a complex."

"Sorry. It's not you. It's me. You remember that messy divorce I told you about…" I intentionally let my voice trail off.

"Yeah. I get it that you're gun shy. But I assure you my intentions are honorable."

Not too honorable, I hope.

I told my inner harlot to shut up.

"It's just that I don't know much about you," I said.

He stabbed two more tiny pieces of meat. "What would you like to know?" He popped the beef into his mouth.

"Some relationship history would be nice." *Did I just say that out loud?*

"I thought I told you that I'm divorced too."

"Any kids?"

His face tightened. "Not anymore."

My throat closed. Boy, I'd stepped in it now. "I'm so sorry."

He put down his fork, took a deep breath and then let it out slowly. "He's why I don't talk much about this stuff. He was… is Emmie's son by a previous marriage. Her first husband died while she was pregnant. We'd started the process for me to adopt Davy when things started going south in our marriage. After we split, I had no legal rights, so no visitation."

I was stunned, and clueless about what to say.

He shifted in his chair to pull his wallet out of his back pocket. He extracted a photo from it and passed it across the table to me.

A snaggle-toothed boy, probably about four years old, with dark curly hair, smiled up at me.

Will reached for the photo. "It's been three years. I'm sure he's forgotten me completely by now."

My chest ached. Again I was at a loss.

He leaned back, stared at the ceiling and blew out air. When he dropped his gaze back to me, I couldn't be sure in the dim light, but it looked like his eyes were red-rimmed. "So, since you have a vested interest in the Garrett case, I'll keep you informed, as much as I can, on the investigation."

I was starting to get it that abruptly changing the subject was Will's favorite defense mechanism.

"I went back through the crime scene," he said. "I think there was another woman there, either that morning or the previous night. There were two mugs–"

"Doris," I said under my breath.

"What?"

I cleared my throat. "Doris admitted to me that she was there earlier that morning, uh, talking to Julie."

Will looked a little stunned. Then he shook his head. "Doris?"

I nodded.

"Why didn't she tell me that?"

My stomach clenched, threatening to give back the *poulet*. "Uh, I got the impression they'd had a bit of a spat. You know, friends can…" I trailed off, not so intentionally this time. I truly didn't know what I was trying to say. Only what I was trying *not* to say.

He tapped a finger against his lips. "Maybe they fought over Julie's affair. Doris swore she didn't know who Julie was seeing on the side, but maybe… Seems like I need to have another talk with her. And give the whole crew another lecture on crime scene processing. I can't believe they missed that those mugs weren't clean."

My insides were a mess. "Everybody was sure Jimmy did it," I croaked out.

"Yeah, Frank even called it a slam dunk. And I agreed with him at the time."

"Frank Larson?" I said, stalling.

"Yeah, he was the one who suggested tranquilizing the dog."

His words barely registered. I sat there like a slug, my brain stalled, my body frozen, overwhelmed with guilt. Only I wasn't sure if it was about letting part of Doris's secret slip out or about not telling Will the whole truth.

"I gotta find Julie's lover," he said. "He's the key to all of this."

Then he smiled. "Okay, enough shop talk. Do you want dessert?"

My chest felt like it was in a vise. I really needed to tell him the rest of it. He was going to waste time looking for Doris, when I was pretty sure she wasn't the killer. "No, I'm full," I managed to push past the lump in my throat.

He gestured toward the wine bottle ensconced in an ice bucket.

Knowing better, I nodded. I needed the liquid courage, as my father used to call it. And yes, Episcopalians drink alcohol. We are sometimes referred to as Whiskepalians, although my parents and most of their friends preferred wine. In moderation, of course. Getting plastered was frowned upon.

Will topped off my glass.

I took a healthy swig, bracing myself.

He covered my hand on the table with his own. "Marcia," he said in a soft voice, "I love that name."

My innards melted into a pile of mush. It was all I could do to keep from sliding off my chair.

We stared into each other's eyes for a few seconds. My nether regions were distinctly warm. The heat moved north until my cheeks burned. "Uh, about the–"

Pierre appeared out of nowhere. "Ah, *madame et monsieur*, you have enjoyed your dinner, *non*?"

Will beamed up at him. "Yes, it was excellent."

"You wish ze dessert?" Pierre said.

I shook my head a little too vigorously. All I wanted was to get the heck out of there.

"No, thank you," Will said. "We'll take the check, please."

I gave the restaurant owner a fake smile. "It was delicious."

Will stared at me after Pierre had left. "What's the matter?"

I faked a yawn. "Just tired. It's been a long day."

Pierre was quick with the check. Will paid the bill, with a token protest from me, which he ignored.

As we walked out of the restaurant, he hesitantly took my hand. The tentativeness of the gesture warmed my heart.

We strolled across the parking lot to my car. He dropped my hand and took me by the shoulders. "Marcia," he whispered. He gently pulled me toward him. His lips hovered close to mine.

My inner neurotic panicked. "Doris was her lover," I blurted out.

CHAPTER EIGHTEEN

Will stiffened. His fingers dug into my shoulders. After a beat he said, "How long have you known that?"

I counted back in my head, trying to remember what day I'd had that conversation with Doris. But I couldn't think straight with Will's eyes–now an icy blue–boring into mine. "A few days."

His face had gone blank, a cop's mask. "And when exactly were you planning to tell me?"

I had no good answer to that. I had no answer at all.

I shrugged, trying to loosen his grip. "I'm sorry. She told me all this in confidence, and I didn't think she'd done it."

"Done what?" His voice was sharp.

"Killed Julie?" My own tone was tentative.

He shook his head, then dropped his hands. I got the distinct impression he'd resisted the urge to push me away. "Goodnight, Marcia."

He turned on his heel and walked away from me.

My throat closed. "I'm sorry," I whispered.

I woke up the next morning a hot mess, literally. The oversized tee-shirt that I'd slept in was clammy with sweat. The sheets and blanket were twisted around my legs and feet.

I recalled at least three times that Buddy had planted his front paws on the side of the bed and nudged me with his nose to wake me from bad dreams.

Those dreams had been populated by frowning, hunky sheriffs

and pissed-off, raspy-voiced women. One of the women had been a strange combination of my mother and Doris.

I sucked down a cup of caffeine and decided there wasn't much I could do about the frowning sheriff, but I could apologize to the pissed-off, raspy-voiced woman for telling her secret. I didn't particularly want to but the manners my mother taught me dictated that I suck it up and call her.

I phoned the Collinsville Sheriff's Department. A male voice answered.

"Is Doris there?"

"She called in sick."

"Oh…"

"You wanna leave a message?"

"Uh, who's this?"

"Deputy Larson."

No, I definitely did not want to leave a message with him.

"Uh, do you have Doris's home number?"

"Not allowed to give that out."

Crapola!

"Okay… well… I'll call her tomorrow then."

"Hey, my caller ID says you're that–"

"Thank you, I'll call back later." I disconnected.

As if that will change what he's already seen.

I was screwed!

I grabbed a cold pop tart for breakfast and got online. Then I realized I didn't know Doris's last name.

Okay, as an amateur sleuth, I sucked.

Maybe it was best that I couldn't reach Doris. If I was wrong about her and she did kill Julie, I'd be giving her time to make up a good story before Will Haines got to her house.

Or maybe he'd already been there and that's why she'd called in sick. I felt bad for her. I knew Will would be discreet, not blab her business around town. And I doubted he'd fire her. But I'm not sure she believed that about him.

You don't know that about him either, my obnoxious inner

voice said.

That stopped me cold. I really didn't know that about him. But I liked him, and I wanted him to be a fair person. Therefore, I was assuming he was.

You don't just like him. You've got the hots for him.

"Ah, shut up!" I muttered.

Buddy looked up from where he was lying next to my chair. He gave me his head-tilt, what's-up look.

Another thought slammed into my solar plexus. What if Doris tried to kill herself? My eyes stung. I couldn't handle another suicide on my conscience.

Okay, I'll be the first to admit that I wasn't thinking straight. Guilt and too little sleep do not make for optimal brain functioning.

I was *not* responsible for these people's lives or actions, I told myself. That reminder did nothing to shrink the lump in my throat nor the knot in my stomach.

Why did I even care about Doris? She hadn't been particularly friendly toward me right from the start.

The lumps and knots stayed intact. I was desperate for something I could do to make the situation better.

Miss Shirley! She'd know how to get in touch with Doris.

Of course, I didn't know her last name either. But I knew where she lived. Not the street number but the name of the street at least. I plugged that, her first name and Collinsville, Florida into my search box.

Eureka! Shirley Gladden popped up. I called information and got a phone number.

"Hello." An elderly voice.

"Miss Shirley?"

"Yes."

"This is Marcia Banks. Do you happen to have Doris's phone number? I heard she was sick and I wanted to call and check on her."

A pregnant pause. I probably sounded a bit frantic for someone who only wanted to check on a sick acquaintance.

"I may have it," Miss Shirley finally said. "She goes to my church. I have a directory around here somewhere." Papers rustling. "Here it is." She read off the number.

I wrote it down. "Thanks so much."

"What's wrong with Doris?"

"Uh, I don't know. I just heard that she was sick."

"Tsk, tsk. There's a stomach virus goin' around town. Hope she didn't get that."

I managed to extract myself from the conversation without feeding any more tidbits to the rumor mill. Then I smacked myself on the forehead. I'd just made matters worse. Now the local gossip was curious about Doris.

I punched Doris's number into my phone. It rang, and rang, and rang. No answer. Not even voicemail. Who doesn't have voicemail these days?

Panic set it. I envisioned her lying on the floor, an empty pill bottle in her hand. I started to call the sheriff's department, then thought better of it. There was no way to explain to Deputy Frank why I thought Doris might be suicidal without revealing her secret to him. And I definitely didn't want to talk to Will Haines.

Should I call Miss Shirley back and ask her to check on Doris? Yeah, bad idea. I'd already piqued the old gossip's curiosity.

I tried Doris's phone number again. And again it rang and rang.

The urge was growing to get in the car and go down there. But it was long drive just to seek absolution and if Doris really had done something to herself, my arrival two or more hours later wouldn't accomplish much.

A little voice suggested that it wasn't Doris's absolution I was seeking. I really wanted Will Haines to forgive me. I fantasized arriving at Doris's door just in time to save her, and then comforting Will when he blamed himself. My sin of omission would be inconsequential next to his guilt for triggering the woman's suicide attempt.

I snorted. "Get a grip, Banks," I said out loud.

Buddy raised his head and tilted it in the other direction. I dubbed his expression the Mom's-losing-it look.

Okay, bottom line was that I was going to go crazy if I didn't find out what was going on in Collinsville. And the only person I could call and ask directly was Will Haines, who already knew Doris's secret and would know what I was talking about.

Yeah, I wasn't about to make *that* call. So long drive it was.

I considered taking Buddy but decided I would have more flexibility without him along.

I let the dogs out to do their business. Then I topped off their water dishes and put Lacy in her crate. I debated about putting Buddy in Max's crate but decided against it.

If someone tried to break in, a barking eighty-pound dog on the other side of the door was much more of a deterrent than one locked in a crate.

I left Buddy loose in the house and headed out to my car.

As I drove, I prayed I wasn't bringing more unfriendly reptiles into our lives by showing up in Collinsville.

By the time I got there, my stomach was letting me know that one pop tart was wholly inadequate nutrition. Also, my little pea brain had realized that physically being in Collinsville brought me no closer to knowing where to find Doris.

I was mentally slapping myself for not asking Miss Shirley for Doris's last name. But then again, that would have seemed weird, that I knew Doris well enough to be concerned when she was sick but didn't know her last name.

I'd have to risk it and go to the diner. The Collinsville phone book hadn't been very big. I could skim down the pages. How many people named Doris were likely to live here anyway?

My stomach growled again. While I was at it, I could get an egg sandwich to go.

I walked into the restaurant and stopped by the cash register, under the sign marked *Carryout.* There weren't many patrons mid-morning and Jane stood next to one of several men seated at a table about halfway between me and the phone booth.

She glanced my way and pursed her lips. The man next to her turned around.

I groaned inside. Why wasn't Deputy Frank still back at the sheriff's department answering the phones?

I really, really didn't want to walk past them to get to the phone booth.

Jane took a step in my direction. "What do you want?" Her tone was far from welcoming.

The deputy snickered. The two other men at the table looked uncomfortable.

I bit back the snarky response that came to mind.

Bees, honey, remember?

"Something to eat," I said as evenly as I could muster. But then the snarky me took over. "This is an eating establishment, isn't it?"

Jane sneered, hunching her shoulders like an aggressive dog. The movement made her too-tight uniform ride up a little. It showed off every bulge.

For a moment, I felt sorry for her. She wasn't all that overweight and she was well-proportioned. If she'd wear clothes that fit properly, she'd be attractive. That is, if she lost the sour expression.

I was beginning to think she was going to ignore my request for food. Another waitress came out of the kitchen, carrying a large tray full of plates. She was as petite as Jane was bulgy, with medium brown skin and short, wavy black hair. She delivered the plates to the men at the table.

Jane said something in a low voice, then jerked her head in my direction.

The other waitress looked from Jane to me and back again. Then she came my way. She must have noticed that I was gritting my teeth, because she leaned in close. "Don't take it personal. Jane's mean to just about everybody." She glanced over her shoulder. "Exceptin' Deputy Larson."

Jane had her back to us, her hand resting on Frank's shoulder.

"They've got a thing going?" I asked in a low voice.

"No," the waitress whispered back. "But Jane wishes they did." Then she giggled, her eyes sparkling.

I smiled at her. "Thanks. You're a bright spot in an otherwise lousy morning."

She flashed a big grin. "Glad to be of service. Now can I get ya somethin' to eat?"

"A fried egg and bacon sandwich to go, please. And do you happen to know where Doris lives? The receptionist from over at the sheriff's office."

"Sure. She lives in her daddy's old house, over on Starke Street."

Didn't anybody ever move into their own place in this town? Seemed like they were all living in their ancestors' houses. "You know the number?"

"Not off the top of my head, but it's the big brown house, two doors down off of Main Street."

"Thanks." I waited uncomfortably for my sandwich, feeling like a bug under a microscope every time Deputy Frank glanced my way. Jane had disappeared.

Then she was back, carrying a khaki uniform shirt on a hanger. "Got that tear all darned up for ya, Frank," she said brightly.

I realized my mouth was hanging open and closed it. Frank glanced my way again. I quickly looked away. It wouldn't do for him to realize that I knew the significance of that tear.

But then again, what was its significance? Deputy Frank might have helped with tranquilizing Buddy or with getting him to Will's car. There were too many logical explanations for how his sleeve could have caught on Buddy's collar buckle.

The young waitress returned, carrying a small white bag. She leaned toward me as she handed it over. "I gave ya some extra bacon."

I thanked her and dug in my purse for money to pay the bill, plus a hefty tip.

"Hey, you're that dog trainer, aren't you? The one that took the Garretts' dog."

My surprised look elicited another giggle. "Honey, there ain't no such thing as a secret in a small town."

I grinned back. "I know. I live in one even smaller than Collinsville." I said goodbye, stealing one more glance at Frank Larson. Then I headed back to my car.

Eating with one hand while steering with the other, I drove slowly through town, reading street signs. I'd forgotten to ask which direction to take on Starke, but it turned out to only go off to the right. I rolled around the corner and pulled up in front of the only big brown house in sight.

No one answered my knock on the front door. I banged a little louder. Still no response. Panic was returning. My stomach clenched. Was I really going to find her dead on the floor?

Bacon-flavored bile rose in the back of my throat. I swallowed and walked across the porch to the nearest window. Cupping my hands around the sides of my face, I peered in to each of the front windows. Dark, unoccupied rooms, but devoid of any corpses.

I knocked again. Still no answer.

I stepped off the porch and walked around the side of the house. The windows here were too far off the ground for me to see in. I went around back and knocked on that door. Nothing happened.

I moved over to a window that was lower than the others and stood on tiptoe to see in. I was looking at a dark kitchen. Again no corpses in sight.

"What the devil are you doin'?"

I whirled around, heart pounding.

CHAPTER NINETEEN

Doris stood in the back doorway, one hand on her hip, the other holding the front of a bathrobe closed.

My knees turned to jelly. "Crapola, Doris. You scared the bejeezus out of me."

"I scared you! Seems like you're the one sneakin' around my backyard, peekin' in my windows."

"I was worried about you when you didn't answer your phone or your door." Now that I was standing here with her in front of me, obviously quite alive, I felt downright foolish.

"*You* were worried about *me*. Since when?"

"Well, I…" Suddenly my eyes were stinging and a lump the size of a basketball had planted itself in my throat. My shoulders began to shake. I sobbed out, "I can't handle… another… suicide."

I couldn't believe I was crying in front of this woman. I gritted my teeth, trying to stop, but my chest still heaved.

"You'd best come in 'fore the neighbors hear ya."

Suddenly wary, I took a hesitant step forward. What if this woman was a killer?

What if Will Haines comes by and sees you blubbering?

That propelled me through the door behind Doris. We entered the dim kitchen.

She flipped the light switch, then grabbed a box of tissues from the counter and tossed them on the table. Her movements were brusque, but her eyes were soft, her mouth down-turned.

I swiped at my eyes and tried to get control of myself, before Doris decided to join me. This was not a woman I wanted to share a cry fest with.

"Have you seen Will since last night?" I wiped away the last of the tears, which I now realized were mostly about Jimmy, with some grief over lost opportunities with Will thrown in.

One of her eyebrows arched. "Oh, so it's *Will* now. Yeah, he stopped by this mornin'."

Phew, so she already knew and she was still being nice to me, or what passed for nice with Doris.

"I'm sorry. I had to tell him," I said. "He was going to waste time looking for Julie's lover because he thinks that's who killed her."

Both eyebrows flew up. "You *told* him?"

"Yeah. Wait, he didn't…? You said he came by this morning."

"He did. I was tossin' my cookies at the time he knocked. By the time I got to the door he was gettin' back in his car. I didn't really feel up for company so I let him go. Figured he'd come back or call later."

"Look, I don't know Will Haines well yet." Her eyebrows arched again at the *yet*. "But I don't think he's the type to discriminate, or to blab other people's business around town."

She snorted. "Obviously you haven't lived in a small town."

I wanted to say that I had, but the two years I'd been in Mayfair didn't really stack up against Doris's several decades. I'd spent most of my life in the suburbs of Baltimore where it took six months for you to learn your immediate neighbors' names.

"It's like a wildfire," Doris was saying. "One person finds out. That's the match bein' struck. Even if they swear not to say nothin', somehow it spreads like crazy from there."

I recalled the words of the waitress at the diner, *No such thing as a secret in a small town.*

I apologized again. Doris waved a hand at me. I wasn't sure what that meant but I didn't push it. She got up and led me to her front door. Then she stopped in her tracks.

She poked her chin toward the window in the door. "Sheriff's department cruiser."

Crapola! Will Haines was here.

I was screwed.

Doris let me sneak out the back. I slipped along the side of the house and peeked around the corner.

It wasn't Will in the car. It was a much bulkier silhouette. Frank Larson.

I turned and walked in the other direction, which unfortunately was away from my car. I'd have to wait until the deputy left before I could retrieve it.

I wandered around that section of town, trying not to draw people's attention. On a side street just off of Main, I spotted Will coming toward me.

My heart stuttered a bit in my chest. I didn't think he'd seen me. I turned to walk the other way.

And practically ran into John Collins. My pulse jolted into overdrive.

"I thought I told you to stay outta this town." His red face was just inches from mine.

Okay, that pissed me off. I leaned a little closer still. "Looks to me like I'm on a public sidewalk."

Collins took a half step back. "Well, we'll see how cocky you are, when I take that dog away from you. He's my niece's and I want him. He's worth a lot of money."

My throat closed. I felt the blood draining out of my face. Dizzy, I took a step back myself. I was really glad I'd decided not to bring Buddy with me. "You can't do that," I stammered.

"We'll see about that." The sheriff's voice from behind, firm and cold.

For one awful moment, I thought he was on Collins' side.

Then he put a hand on my shoulder. Warmth spread from it down to my toes, leaving a trail of tingly feelings.

"Possession is nine-tenths of the law," Will said. "You'll have to take Ms. Banks to court to get the animal."

Inspiration struck. "Jimmy gave him to me, before he died."

"He put it in writing?" Collins said.

I didn't say anything, because of course he hadn't. He hadn't really given him to me, although he sort of did when he asked me to take care of him. The unspoken implication had been I would do so permanently should Jimmy go to prison.

Collins snorted, then a grin grew slowly across his face. "I didn't think so. We've only got your word on that. We'll see what a judge has to say."

He pivoted and marched away.

I turned to Will, a grateful smile on my face. It faded at the sight of the storm clouds on his.

"I told you to stay away from Collinsville. Do you have a death wish?"

"Uh…" I had to think fast. I wasn't about to tell him that I'd come to see Doris. "I wanted to apologize to you."

"You could've called."

"I felt it required an in-person apology."

"Humph. Come on. I'll walk you to your car."

I tried not to let my panic show. *Think fast, Banks!*

"Uh, I parked it on a side street, you know, trying to keep a low profile. Uh, now I can't remember where I left it."

I scolded myself internally for all the *uh's*. I sure sounded like a liar to my own ears.

"You got a panic button on your key fob?"

'Hey, why didn't I think of that?" I gave him a bright smile. I pulled out the fob and hit the button. My car started bleeping the next block over.

Will nodded brusquely. "Come on." He took my elbow. "I was headed that way anyway."

When we turned the corner onto Starke Street, the first thing I saw was no sheriff's department cruiser. Deputy Frank was gone.

The second thing I saw was Doris lounging in a wicker chair on her front porch.

I gently pulled loose from Will's grasp. "I gotta get going.

Thanks for rescuing me from Collins." I should've shut up at that point, but no, I kept right on blabbering. "We still on for the basketball game on Saturday?"

He had taken a step past me. Now he stopped and turned on his heel. The expression on his face was unreadable. He stared at me for a beat. "Not sure. I'll call you."

He turned back around and headed for Doris's house.

I jumped in my car and got the heck out of there as fast as I could.

Worry over Buddy churned in my stomach as I drove. John Collins had deep pockets, and I pretty much had no pockets. If he took me to court, I was royally screwed.

I was going to lose Buddy.

CHAPTER TWENTY

Twenty minutes down the road, I pulled over on the shoulder. My mind had been scrambling for something to think about, to distract me from my fears about Buddy. It had landed on Carol Reynolds, the scowling admin at the bank.

"You're not supposed to be investigating," I said out loud.

My vision blurred as I flashed back to the last time I'd talked to Jimmy Garrett before Julie was murdered. It was when I'd called to follow up on how he and Buddy were getting along. He'd reassured me that they were doing fine.

"Uh, the only glitch is when my wife and I, you know…" I'd imagined Jimmy's tanned and rugged cheeks blushing. "But we solved that by putting him out in the living room while we're…"

To fill the awkward silence, I said, "I'll bet he whines the whole time."

A chuckle had come across the phone line. "Yeah, but we've gotten used to tuning him out."

I blinked hard. A tear trickled down my cheek. I swiped impatiently at it with the back of my hand.

Despite Julie's infidelity, the Garretts had been good people, and they'd loved each other. They didn't deserve to be dead.

You're gonna blow it with the sheriff.

I pointed out to my inner voice that I probably already had, and John Collins had assumed I'd come to Collinsville to poke my nose into things again.

There are no secrets in a small town.

The killer would know by dinnertime that I'd been there and would make the same assumption.

I dug through my purse for the piece of paper with the Reynolds woman's address on it. Then I glanced at my watch. I could easily get there before she got home from work. If I could get past her animosity, maybe I could determine if the thing Julie was checking out had anything to do with the bank.

My GPS kept trying to take me back through Collinsville, but I finally convinced it there was a traffic jam, and it gave me an alternate route via back roads. I went through a fast food drive-thru on the outskirts of Polk City to get some lunch. At a little after two, I arrived at the address that I hoped was the home of the correct Carol Reynolds. I figured I had at least an hour to kill before she got there.

As soon as it didn't have something else to distract it, my mind veered back to thoughts of losing Buddy. My stomach churned, threatening to give back the Big Mac I'd just wolfed down.

Maybe I should call Mattie. I had a vague recollection of some kind of clause in the clients' contracts that said the service animal reverted back to the organization in the event of the veteran's death. And I still hadn't asked her about protocols for training mentor dogs or if anyone had tried something similar to my Lassie response before.

I had my phone out and was about to place the call when another thought had my stomach flipping over again. My fingers froze above the numbers. That reversion clause would keep Buddy out of John Collins' hands, but I would still lose him.

I was fighting back tears when a car pulled into the driveway of the house I was watching. Sure enough, Collins' admin assistant stepped out of it. She glanced furtively over her shoulder. Did she sense me watching from across the street?

I ducked down some in my car and looked at my watch. It was only two-thirty. The bank didn't close until three.

Once she was inside, I got out of my own car and walked up to her front door. I took a deep breath and rang the doorbell.

The door swung open almost immediately. "You're early…" Her eyes went wide. "Oh!"

"May I come in?" I nudged the door open further and stepped past her before she had a chance to react.

She scowled at me. "Get out!"

I pointed to the door. "You might want to close that," I said with a calmness I wasn't really feeling. "Wouldn't want to advertise to your neighbors all about your affairs."

The word "affairs" was an educated guess. Ms. Reynolds was not wearing a ring on her left hand, and there was no easy chair in her small living room, just a short couch across from the TV. She was single, yet she had been expecting someone. And she'd come home early to meet him.

Or her. I reminded myself that, after Doris's revelations, I shouldn't be taking anything for granted.

She slammed the door and turned on me. "What do you want?"

Wow, this woman had even worse anger issues than I did. What had I ever done to her, other than pretend to be someone I wasn't with her boss?

"I happened to be in the area and thought I'd drop by."

Her narrowed eyes said she wasn't buying that. I really hadn't expected her to.

"Why the evil eye?" I said. "What'd I ever do to you?"

Her face went blank. No doubt, she hadn't been expecting such a blunt confrontation. Then she drew herself up and looked down her nose at me. "I don't like people who tell lies."

I snorted.

She scowled.

This was getting nowhere fast.

"Look, I'm just trying to figure out who really killed your boss's sister, because I don't believe her husband did it." Okay, I probably shouldn't have said that since I wasn't supposed to be investigating anymore.

The eyes were narrowed again. "You're one of those

bleeding-heart liberals, aren't you?"

I stifled a sigh as I noted that her accent was Northern. I tried to keep the anger out of my voice, but with little success. "Since when is caring about our country's veterans a liberal or conservative issue?"

Her mouth made a small o.

I resisted the urge to smirk. She didn't have a good answer for that. I pressed my advantage. "How did Julie act at the bank? Was she anxious about anything? Preoccupied? Did she have any enemies there?"

Carol Reynolds's lip curled for a second, before she caught herself. "No, she didn't have enemies," she said, in a too-sweet voice. "Most people liked her."

"Most people, but not everybody?"

Her eyes darted back and forth from my face to various parts of the room. "No, everybody did."

"So how did she and her brother get along?"

"Fine, they got along fine." She let out a fake chuckle. "Oh, they had their moments, a little sibling rivalry now and again." Her gaze darted to the door.

Her lover was due soon and that was making her nervous. Maybe she'd let something slip. "Folks around town say that John really didn't like her."

Her face morphed into a mask of fury. "She just pushed herself in there! Everything was fine until their grandmother died."

She stopped, wiped the anger from her expression. "John resented her some, but basically they got along."

Wow! Talk about Dr. Jekyll and Ms. Hyde. I struggled not to let it show that I didn't believe her.

"Was there anything going on at the bank," I asked again, "that Julie might have been worried about?"

She looked at me as if I'd spoken the question in Chinese, then she shook her head.

Time to leave. I doubted I'd get more out of her, and her lover would be here soon. I had a sneaking suspicion who he was and didn't particularly want to come face to face with him.

I thanked her for her time and made for the door. Again, she had that o-mouth thing going. She looked like a startled fish.

Once in my car, I moved it down the block a ways. I'd no sooner put my transmission in park than a car pulled into Ms. Reynolds's driveway.

A man stepped out of the car, his back to me. He walked to the front door, but didn't ring the doorbell. Instead he knocked lightly.

Then he turned so his profile was visible. As I'd suspected, it was John Collins.

CHAPTER TWENTY-ONE

The long drive from Polk City gave me plenty of time to contemplate what all that meant. Had Julie discovered John's affair? Since she herself had been unfaithful in her marriage, I found it hard to believe she would be "preoccupied" because of her brother's infidelity.

Had John discovered that Julie knew about his affair and killed her to keep her from telling his wife? I also had trouble envisioning Sheila Collins breaking up her family over an affair. She was more the look-the-other-way type.

But John might be worried about his reputation if the affair got out.

I shook my head as I drove. The majority of the bank's big depositors were most likely men, and they probably wouldn't hold a little hanky-panky on the side against him.

No, I couldn't see any way that John's affair gave him a strong motive for murder. But… I recalled that flash of irrational fury on Carol's face.

Working in the bank every day with his sister must have been beyond tense for John. Had girlfriend Carol decided to eliminate the major thorn in her lover's side?

Yeah, that I could believe!

Now the question was how to get this info to the sheriff. Coming from me, I knew it would not be well received.

I rummaged in my purse for my phone.

"Hey, Doris."

She was barely civil but she promised to pass on the information as a rumor she'd heard around town.

By the time I got home, I was famished–and exhausted. Emotional roller coaster rides apparently burned up a lot of energy.

I made a peanut butter and banana sandwich and sat down at the table with it to call Becky. I might as well rename her Mother Confessor. "So do you think I've completely blown it with him?" I asked, after filling her in on the encounter with Will, and his cryptic response to my question about our Saturday date.

I hadn't told her about the whole losing Buddy issue. I didn't want to think about it right now.

"Hmm. No," Becky said, "not completely, or else Sheriff Hunky would've just cancelled. Sounds like he's working on getting over being mad at you."

I said a short, silent prayer that he'd never find out I'd been the one who'd discovered John Collins' affair.

Becky's words had sparked a tiny glimmer of hope in my chest. It didn't give off much warmth. And I wasn't sure if I wanted to gently blow on it and nurse it into a stronger flame, or stomp it out.

I sighed into the phone. "This is why I avoid dating. The beginning of a relationship is so nerve-racking."

Becky laughed. "That's because you take it so seriously. If you don't care, you can just have fun."

I remained silent. Becky had her own failed love affair, although it hadn't made it to marriage status before it blew up on her. For the first time, I realized that her casual, devil-may-care attitude toward men was her own defense mechanism.

I changed the subject. "Hey, you got any window of time tomorrow to help me again with Lacy?"

She did and we set it up for three the next afternoon.

After I'd signed off, I checked in with the little flame in my chest. It was still flickering, giving off a tepid glow of hope.

While I fed and watered the dogs, I mulled over whether I

should try to find out more about the town council, Deputy Frank and that Dwayne what's-his-name. My three main sources of information in Collins up to this point had been the sheriff, Miss Shirley and Doris. The sheriff was out, obviously. And if I talked to Miss Shirley, the conversation would not stay private. So I'd need to stick to Doris for now.

But the bigger question was whether I should keep asking anybody questions about anything. If word got back to the killer that I was still investigating, he–or she, let's not forget the angry admin–would probably sic something worse than a teenaged reptile on me.

And if the sheriff found out, he'd probably never speak to me again. Becky thought he was going to come around in time. I wasn't sure I wanted to screw that up.

I decided to think about it tomorrow.

I flopped down on the sofa, clicked on the TV and brought up my Netflix queue. I watched an episode of *Orange Is the New Black*, while pretending that I wasn't waiting for the phone to ring.

By the next morning, the little ember of hope in my chest had turned to a small, cold stone.

To distract myself, I decided to at least call Doris and get the names of the town council members and pump her for more on Collins' friends.

I called the sheriff's department and Doris answered. I let out the breath I'd been holding. As I'd suspected, the sheriff hadn't fired her.

"How are you feeling?" I said quickly, before she had a chance to hang up on me.

"Better." Her voice was more gravelly and terse than usual.

"Look, I need to know more about Frank Larson and that other guy, Dwayne…" I couldn't remember his last name. Like I said, I suck as an amateur sleuth.

"Snyder."

So this is the way it's going to be. I stifled a sigh.

"Tell me about him." There, that would force her to give me more than a one-word answer.

She gave me four. "Loner. Not real bright."

"Loner? I thought you said he was friends with John Collins?"

"As close to friendship as Dwayne's able to do."

"How about John and Frank? Are they tight or more casual friends?"

"They're pretty tight." She dropped her voice. "He's not the brightest bulb in the package either. Sheriff Haines inherited him from the previous sheriff."

"Tell me more. Are they married, single?"

"Frank's divorced. Don't think Dwayne ever even talks to women, 'less he has to."

"He's that shy?"

"Not shy," she said. "More a recluse. I think he's got a touch of that newfangled disorder everybody's talkin' about, the one that's related to autism."

"Asperger's?"

"Yeah, that's it."

"How about violent tendencies?"

"Naw, he's not dangerous."

I meant both of them. Doris was now answering me in complete sentences, but apparently I still had to ask the right questions.

"And Frank?"

"He's a little hung up on the power of bein' a deputy." Again the lowered voice. "But he's mostly bark. There's never been any complaints filed against him for bein' rough with people."

"How about the town council? Who's on it?"

A pause.

"Look, I thought you wanted me to find out who really killed Julie."

"I'll email you a list, with some background info."

I gave her my email address. She repeated it back to me.

I'd run out of things to ask. "Uh, thanks."

Doris didn't bother to say goodbye, just disconnected.

Later I would realize I had forgotten one very important question.

CHAPTER TWENTY-TWO

Over lunch, I tried to remember if I'd ever told Will Haines about the tear in Deputy Frank's uniform. I debated using Doris again as my go-between, but decided to use this as an excuse to text the sheriff.

He responded a few seconds later with *Thx*.

That's all? The small, cold stone grew to the size of a boulder in my chest.

I dropped the remainder of my sandwich on my plate and shuffled out back to work on reinforcing some of Lacy's basic skills.

The training session with Becky later that afternoon was a repeat of the previous one. I hadn't called Mattie yet–I was procrastinating, afraid of what she would say about the possession of Buddy issue–so we were still winging it with the Lassie response. For now, I wanted to reinforce the first two steps with Lacy, that she was to run away and approach a passerby.

I left Buddy in the house, his nose pressed against the wire mesh of the screen door. He whined softly off and on, clearly unhappy to be excluded from the goings-on.

After forty-five minutes of working with Lacy, I called for a break, signaling to the dog that she was off duty. I let Buddy out and grabbed a chair from the kitchen to replace the more mangled of the bistro chairs. Becky and I settled at the little table on the deck with glasses of iced tea, the dogs at our feet.

An idea popped into my head. After we'd finished our drinks, I put Lacy in her crate inside and sent Becky out to the street with some additional instructions.

"Run, Buddy!" I made the shooing gesture with my hand.

He took off through the open gate, and then I heard Becky saying, "What is it, boy? Where's your owner?"

I walked over to the gate to peek out.

A soft woof from Buddy, then he trotted ahead of Becky, looking back over his shoulder to make sure she was following.

Just as I'd suspected, he had caught on to what I was trying to teach Lacy to do. Not too surprising. He was more highly trained than she, programmed to try to figure out what was expected of him. Whereas Lacy was still mostly in it for the treats.

When Becky came through the gate after Buddy, she was smiling. "*He* gets it, at least."

"Basically," I said. "Most strangers would be a bit resistant to following a stray dog. But I'm thinking we work with him to perfect this maneuver, then he can show Lacy what's expected of her."

"Sounds like a plan, 'cause honestly I can't imagine how we'd convey to her the next part any other way."

I grinned at Becky. She wasn't a trainer but she'd helped me enough as my back-up person that she'd developed a feel for how the whole process worked. Everything had to be broken down into small steps, each step reinforced again and again.

She returned my grin, then glanced at her watch. "Hey, I need to get home. I've got a date tonight. Speaking of which, have you heard from the sheriff?"

I shook my head. "I think I did blow it completely."

Becky patted my shoulder. "Then it wasn't meant to be."

I gritted my teeth to keep from shrugging off her hand. I knew she meant well, was trying to cheer me up, but I hated that platitude. It was the New Age version of "It's God's will." Who knew what the universe put forth with good intentions, only to have us humans screw it up?

Becky and I said our goodbyes and I took the dogs back inside the house. I picked up my cell phone, which I'd left on the counter hooked to its charger, and discovered I had a message.

It was from Will Haines. My heart stuttered a bit in my chest. The little ember of hope glowed softly.

"Hey, Marcia. Sorry this is so last minute but I have an answer finally about tomorrow. I'm afraid the game is off."

The ember dropped into my stomach and sizzled out. I'd really and truly blown it.

"My friend's business trip fell through, so now he and his son are using the tickets. But I'd still like to get together tomorrow afternoon, if you're willing. Maybe catch a movie or go on a picnic or something…" His voice trailed off for a beat. "Uh, let me know."

My head spinning from emotional whiplash, I quickly called him back. And got his voicemail. I left a message saying a picnic sounded good and did he want to pick me up about noon? I'd provide the food.

Once I'd disconnected, I decided it was probably for the best that I'd gotten voicemail. Talking with Will on the phone right now would be awkward. Better to be face to face when I apologized again for not telling him sooner about Doris.

Humming to myself, I headed for the bathroom and a much needed shower. My phone pinged on the bathroom vanity counter while I was luxuriating under the hot water.

Apparently, Will preferred to avoid phone contact as well. He'd texted that a picnic the next day would be great.

I woke up the next morning feeling better than I had in days. I let the dogs out, then fed them and freshened their water dishes.

It briefly crossed my mind to follow up on the town council members, but I shut down that line of thought. I'd made a decision. I was *not* going to jeopardize the possibility of something good between me and Will Haines.

I grabbed a pop tart to eat in the car and headed for the Publix in Belleview for the makings of a date-worthy picnic.

My phone buzzed halfway there, and the name on my caller

ID took some of the bounce out of my happy mood. I swallowed hard and answered. "Hey, Mattie. How's it going?"

A brief pause. "Never can get used to people already knowin' it's me."

I chuckled softly.

"What's the news on the Garrett case?" she asked.

"Uh, what do you mean?"

"Well, is he still in jail? When's the trial?"

Crapola! She hadn't heard about Jimmy's suicide.

My vision blurred as I told her. I blinked back the tears.

Another pause. I visualized Mattie on the other end of the line, digesting it all–her mostly gray hair pulled back in a careless ponytail, her weathered face frowning.

"So Buddy's still with you?" she finally said.

"Yeah, but Jimmy's brother-in-law is threatening to sue to get him back, says he belongs to his niece, but I think he just wants to sell Buddy." I choked a little on the last few words and decided I'd better pull off on the shoulder before I had an accident. My tires crunched on the gravel as I slowed to a stop.

My memory had been correct. Mattie assured me that the clause in the contract clients signed had been carefully vetted by the organization's lawyer. With Jimmy gone, Buddy reverted back to their ownership.

I was relieved that John Collins wouldn't be getting his greedy hands on Buddy, but my heart ached at the thought of giving him up. "Uh, remember you suggested I should train a mentor dog? Buddy's been really helpful with my other dogs. He's already figured out what's expected of him, to show them what to do and all…"

Mattie sighed into the phone. "Marcia, you know I'd like to give him to you, but the board would never go for that. Buddy's still young. They'll want him assigned to another veteran."

"Would they let me buy him?" The words were out of my mouth before they had completely formed in my mind.

Another pause.

I said a silent prayer that one, she'd say yes, and two, I'd miraculously find some way to come up with the money.

"I'll see what I can do." As was her way, Mattie disconnected without saying goodbye.

I hadn't gotten a chance to ask her about the Lassie response, but that could wait. I'd call her Monday. Right now I had a picnic to put together. I tossed my phone on the passenger seat and put the car in gear.

The grocery store was crowded, it being Saturday morning. Who knew this many people lived in Belleview and the surrounding towns? I kept saying "Excuse me," as I bumped into the carts, and sometimes the elbows or butts of fellow shoppers.

While examining the gourmet cheeses, I thought I heard the rumble of a familiar voice. I looked around, then heard it again, coming from the direction of the small group of tables near the deli counter.

I craned my neck to see past the folks standing in line to get their weekly supply of cold cuts and salads. I caught a glimpse of blue chambray.

A couple of people were resistant to letting me and my cart through the line. I guess they thought I was trying to butt in ahead of them. When I finally got to a spot where I had a clear view of the tables, there was no sign of the man I thought I'd heard and seen–my date for that afternoon, Will Haines.

But when I saw the man who *was* sitting at one of the tables, I let out a little yelp.

Fortunately, the crowd of people was making enough noise that the man didn't seem to hear me.

He picked up a paper coffee cup and drained it. Then he rose and walked to a nearby trash can, giving me a good look at his profile. My eyes had not been deceiving me. I knew that profile.

It was John Collins.

As I started for home, I tried to figure out what Collins was doing in the Publix in Belleview on a Saturday morning. It was thirty minutes northwest of my house, and Collinsville was almost two hours south of me, in the opposite direction. Had I imagined another man sitting with him, in a blue shirt and with the deep timber of the sheriff's voice?

Maybe it had been Frank Larson with him. I couldn't imagine a single reason why Will would meet Collins that far from home. Unless it was an accidental encounter. That was a possibility. Will didn't seem to like Collins much, but he'd probably stop to say hello. As an elected official, he couldn't afford to blatantly snub an important citizen of his town.

My phone pinged on the seat next to me, announcing a missed call. I picked it up and checked caller ID. I didn't recognize the number. Probably a telemarketer. I'd check later to see if they'd left a message.

The crowded store and lingering over the gourmet cheeses had caused me to get home later than intended. I grabbed my phone and purse and gathered up the groceries from the backseat.

I juggled plastic bags around to unlock the front door, then dropped them and my purse on the sofa. Lacy huddled in the corner of her crate, but I'd left Buddy loose in the house. Where was he?

I glanced at my grandmother's mantel clock perched to one side of the TV. Yikes, eleven-fifteen already.

Deciding that getting myself ready before Will arrived was more important than having the picnic completely prepared, I left the groceries where I'd dropped them and bolted for the bathroom. "Hey, Buddy, where are you, boy?"

I took the fastest shower of my life, then started to blow my hair dry. I glanced at the open doorway, wondering why Buddy hadn't stuck his head in yet to see what I was up to. Frowning in the mirror at my Medusa impression, I tried to remember where I'd put my flat iron. I rummaged through the cabinet under the sink. No flat iron.

And still no Buddy.

Worry fluttered in my chest. I felt a little queasy.

Grabbing my discarded shirt up off the floor, I wrapped it around me and stepped out into the hall. No Buddy curled up on the hallway rug, his favorite spot to observe the crazy antics involved in his mom getting bathed, coiffed and dressed.

"Buddy?" I scooped up my jeans from the bathroom floor and jogged into the living room.

Belatedly, I noticed that Lacy was trembling in her crate. Hair standing at attention on my neck, I tiptoed toward the corner leading into the kitchen, my jeans crumpled in a death-grip in my hand.

I flicked the jeans' legs around the corner and then jumped back, expecting a four-hundred-pound lizard to snap at the denim. Nothing happened.

"Buddy? Where are you, boy?" My voice was shaky, as was my whole body at this point.

I decided it was time to put the jeans on, in case I had to run for my life. I was halfway through this process when it dawned on me that a creature, four or two-legged, might come out of the kitchen at any second. I panicked and lost my balance, falling sideways onto the armchair. It slipped off the pile of books subbing for a leg and listed to one side.

Head dangling upside down, I yanked the jeans the rest of the way on and buttoned the waist without bothering to zip them. I rolled out of the lopsided chair onto my knees, then jumped to my feet.

A lead brick of dread had taken up residence in my stomach. Something had happened to my dog. I couldn't put off going into the kitchen any longer. It was the only room I hadn't been in since coming home.

I lifted one of the heftier textbooks from the improvised-chair-leg pile and crept to the corner again. I held my breath and peeked around it.

The kitchen seemed to be empty. "Buddy?"

I listened. The house was quiet, except for the ticking of the mantel clock behind me.

I moved slowly into the kitchen, eyes darting from one corner to another. No gator, no human. And no Buddy.

Totally freaked, I checked the locks on the doors, then methodically searched the house. On my second pass through the kitchen, I saw it.

A sheet of white paper, anchored under my peanut butter jar in the middle of the table.

CHAPTER TWENTY-THREE

My heart stuttered in my chest as I read the block letters a second time. They weren't very neat, but the message was loud and clear.

IF YOU WANT TO SEE YOUR DOG ALIVE AGAIN, COME TO 10221 SE HWY 314. ALONE. DON'T TELL NO ONE. BY 1 O'CLOCK OR THE MUTT DIES.

My hand shook, rattling the paper. Someone had invaded my home, again. How had they gotten in?

My mind flashed back to earlier that morning. In my excitement, had I taken the time after I'd closed the front door to stick the key in the deadbolt keyhole to throw that lock? Or, through rote habit, had I just turned the lock on the knob and pulled the door closed behind me?

I was pretty darn sure I hadn't flipped the alarm switch on, since I hadn't had to switch it off when I came home.

Crapola! What time is it?

In a panic, I bolted into the living room. It was eleven-forty. I only had a little over an hour to find this address I'd never heard of, and then figure out how to retrieve Buddy from his dognappers.

I shoved my feet into an old pair of sandals by the door, grabbed my purse and ran from the house. I was halfway down my sidewalk when Mrs. Wells' voice had my feet automatically slowing their pace.

"Marcia!" she called again.

I wanted to ignore her completely–I did *not* have time for

a nosy neighbor–but good manners prevailed, sort of. I turned and walked backwards a few steps. "Sorry, ma'am. I'm in a big hurry." I pivoted and sprinted the last few feet to my car, her strident voice calling my name behind me.

Forty-five minutes later, I was on Highway 314 headed east from Ocala. My GPS hadn't recognized that street number. The closest address it had offered up was 10219. Now, as I was getting closer to it, the little map indicated it was inside the boundaries of the Ocala National Forest.

The saner part of me was yelling, *What the H am I doing?* It was starting to get through to the more impulsive part of me.

I had no business getting anywhere near the Forest, unarmed and by myself, even if it was a bright and sunny Saturday. Edna Mayfair had told me stories of campers and hikers disappearing in there, never to be seen nor heard from again.

I loved Buddy, but I seriously doubted the author of that note had a friendly chat in mind. Getting myself killed wasn't going to help my dog.

I decided to ignore the "don't tell no one" instructions in the note and call Will. Hopefully, he would know what to do.

I rummaged in my purse on the passenger seat while driving one-handed, but I couldn't find my phone. I patted my jeans' pockets. Flat as pancakes.

I dumped the purse over on the seat and stirred the contents. Definitely no phone. I vaguely remembered dropping it next to the groceries on the sofa.

You're a jerk! I noted that my inner voice had switched from first to second person. It had disowned me. I didn't blame it.

My GPS informed me that I was point nine miles from my destination. I squinted through the windshield. Coming up on my right was a large block building, an old sign in front with indecipherable writing on it, and a parking lot of cracked and crumbling asphalt. Beyond it was an expanse of green field surrounded by a few waving palm trees and spindly Southern pines. The land as far as the eye could see was undeveloped. In the distance, a line of trees marked the edge of the Ocala National Forest.

I pulled into the parking lot and parked in the shade of the old building. I'd just take a moment to calm down and get my bearings, then I'd decide what to do next. One thing was sure, I wasn't going into the Forest by myself, without even a cell phone to connect me to the outside world.

I was on my second deep breath when the sound of an engine rumbling nearby sent adrenaline jolting through my system. A large, mud-splattered, brown pick-up pulled in next to my car. A man–fortyish and rather scruffy-looking–was in the driver's seat, watching me.

I didn't recognize him.

He lowered his passenger window and yelled, "You lost, Miss?"

I lowered my own window and gave him a shaky smile. "Do you happen to know…" I looked down at the mess on my passenger seat, stirred it and found the block-letter note with the address on it. I called over to the man. "10221 SE Highway 314. You know where that is?"

He scratched his stubbled chin, then pointed through his grimy windshield. "That should be jest a little bit up the road, but nothin' round there but fields and trees."

I nodded, disappointed that he wasn't going to be able to help. "Thanks any–"

Knuckles rattled my passenger-side window. I jumped and twisted around in my seat.

Deputy Frank was grinning at me through that window. "Thanks for pullin' off, Miz Banks," he called out through the glass. "Makes things a lot easier."

Frantic, I jammed the car into reverse and looked up in my rearview mirror. John Collins stood ten feet behind my bumper, aiming a shotgun at my head.

I jerked my head back around to the man in the truck. "Help…" died on my lips. He was grinning at me.

CHAPTER TWENTY-FOUR

My thoughts scattered. One weird little part of my brain was gleeful. My gut instincts had said there was something off about Deputy Frank and Brother John. And I'd been right.

Another part of my brain was connecting dots. Dwayne Snyder–the man in the mud-splattered brown truck, Collins and Larson's friend. If only I'd asked Doris what Snyder did for a living. He was the gator farmer who'd tranqed Buddy the morning Julie died, and no doubt had deposited a gator in my living room more recently.

Meanwhile, the part that liked living was desperately scrambling for a course of action. They had me boxed in. I could run down John Collins, but most likely he'd blow my head off in the process.

A little ahead and to my left was a palm tree. Could I jump the curb and squeeze between it and the wall of the building? It was worth a try. I jammed the transmission into drive.

Glass shattered to my right. I jerked away from the sound and the sharp spray of shards against my cheek. My foot slipped off the brake and the car jolted forward.

The block wall of the building raced toward me. I twisted the wheel, a scream erupting from my throat. My front fender bounced off the wall and the car careened into the palm tree. An air bag blew up in my face.

The engine stalled. I heard the hiss of escaping steam from my busted radiator.

My door was ripped open, and strong hands beat back the air bag and dragged me out of the car.

"You stupid bitch!" Deputy Frank cranked an arm back to hit me.

John Collins clamped a hand around his wrist. "No! I don't want any marks on her. It's gotta look like an accident."

Okay, that did not bode well.

My heart was pounding in my chest. I gasped for breath.

"Turn her around," Collins barked.

Dwayne Snyder was standing next to him. He puckered his lips and shot a stream of brown tobacco juice into the weeds sticking out of a crack in the pavement.

I struggled to control my gag response.

"Don't know what y'all have in mind here," Dwayne said. "Jest get my truck back to me later."

He stuck his hand in his pocket and pulled out a pistol.

I froze for a precious moment. He'd sounded like he was distancing himself from his friends' actions, but now he was pointing a gun at me. A beat too late, I kicked out at his gun hand, just as I felt the sting in my shoulder. Within seconds, my legs wobbled.

Larson let me sink down on the crumbling asphalt.

My mind put the pieces together, too late to do any good. The pistol was a dart gun.

Dwayne Snyder had just shot me full of gator tranquilizer.

I woke up face down in the back of the pick-up truck. I vaguely remembered Deputy Frank tying my hands and ankles with strips of cloth.

Collins had said something about not wanting abrasion marks. Then he'd run his hands over my body, patting me down to make sure I was weaponless, and unfortunately phoneless.

I was grateful that it was Collins who'd performed that task, and not Frank. But still I was craving a hot shower with lye soap, despite the oven I was trapped in. The camper top on the pick-up absorbed every ray of the Florida sun. The truck bed stank of gator. I tried not to think about what organisms might be lurking in the thin layer of slime on the floor.

One side of me was warmer than the other. I turned my head to that side.

A black furry object was stretched out next to me.

Buddy!

I wiggled closer and nudged him with my elbow. My stomach clenched when he didn't stir.

Then he whimpered. The sound made my chest ache. Was he hurt, or had he just been tranquilized?

"It's okay, boy," I whispered, even though things were far from okay. "I'm here."

He whimpered again and moved his head slightly.

The pick-up bounced, jarring us around. My bowels turned to liquid. We were no longer on paved road, probably deep within the Ocala National Forest. The sound of water splashing against the side of the truck as we plunged through a stream.

The truck stopped, the cooling engine pinging in the quiet of the woods. The back hatch opened and thick, fumbling fingers untied my ankles. Larson grabbed me around the waist and hauled me out. I stood on shaky legs and watched him lift Buddy out and set him on the ground. The dog pushed awkwardly to his feet and swayed a little.

Larson pulled out his service revolver and aimed it at Buddy.

"No!" I screamed.

Collins thrust his arm out in front of Larson. "We need him as leverage to control her."

I wasn't quite sure how much more "controlling" of me was needed. I was out in the middle of nowhere, my hands tied, and still woozy from the tranquilizer.

Collins waved at me that I should walk ahead of them. I took a couple of wobbly steps and almost fell. Collins made a disgusted sound deep in his throat.

Larson picked me up and threw me over his shoulder in a fireman's carry. He stomped through the underbrush. I lifted my head to check on Buddy.

Collins had him by the collar and was guiding him after us. The dog staggered like a drunk.

My chest ached. My stomach, with Larson's shoulder planted in the middle of it, wasn't particularly happy either. I considered puking down his back, but decided to fight the urge. Best not to provoke the enemy until I had the lay of the land.

The lay of the land was a broken-down shack, a hundred or so feet away from the dirt road and hidden behind a stand of palmettos. Larson stepped carefully over rotted porch boards and an equally rotted threshold. A termite-riddled door hung from one hinge. Very little daylight filtered through the trees, and even less made it through the dirty windows of the shack. Larson waited while Collins lit several kerosene lamps. Then at a gesture from Collins, he flopped me down on a large wooden table.

I struggled to raise my head and see what had happened to Buddy. A glimpse of black fur falling more than lying down on the floor.

"Tie her to the table," Collins said. "We need to find out what she knows and who else she's told about it."

My mind scrambled for a plausible excuse for why I wouldn't have told Will Haines anything that I'd discovered. Too many of those things pointed to Collins and Larson. But I knew I was a wimp. If they tortured me, I'd probably throw Will under the bus, and Doris for good measure.

Then it dawned on me. They weren't going to torture me. They were going to hurt Buddy if I didn't tell.

Larson approached my feet, more cloth strips in hand. Buddy growled. I glanced over. He had stood up, still wobbly but upright.

I cocked my foot back and let it fly.

The satisfying crunch of collapsing cartilage was followed by a howl of pain, and Larson staggered backward. Collins raced to the table and grabbed my ankles.

"Run, Buddy! Run!" I didn't care if he remembered the bring-back-the-rescue-party part of it. It would be too late to do any good anyway. I just wanted him out of there.

Buddy looked at me for a fraction of a second. Then he bolted out the open door.

Collins started after him but came to a halt near the door. Distant sounds of Buddy crashing through the underbrush said he had a good head start.

"Doesn't matter. He'll get eaten by a bear or a gator before he makes it out of the Forest." Collins turned back and smiled, a nasty glint in his eye.

My stomach heaved. I prayed he was wrong.

He walked to where Larson was bent over, making snuffling noises, both hands holding his bleeding nose. He pulled Frank's service revolver from its holster and pointed it at me.

"Who else did you tell about what you found out?"

Fury exploded in my chest, an excellent antidote for fear. "I didn't tell anybody!"

"Give me one good reason why I should believe you?" Collins said.

We went back and forth like that for a good fifteen minutes, with him waving the gun at me and yelling some variation of what did I tell and who did I tell it to.

And me yelling back, "Nothing! Nobody!"

Larson periodically moaned about his broken nose, and Collins told him to shut up.

A couple of times, Collins put the gun under my chin and threatened to blow the top of my head off. That didn't scare me all that much, since he'd already let on that I was to have an accident. What did scare the bejesus out of me was contemplating how he might make that accident happen.

The more red in the face he got as he screamed at me, the more I worried that he'd be sure it was a painful accident.

The crack of a gunshot echoed through the woods.

Collins stopped in mid rant and squinted out a dirty window near him.

It was the best opening I was likely to get. I bolted off the table.

I made it as far as the doorway and smacked into a broad chest. I looked up into familiar blue eyes. My chest swelled with joy. I was saved!

“Well, well, look who’s joined the party.” Collins’ voice, downright jovial, from behind me.

The blank expression on Will’s face registered in my brain, just before he nudged me back into the room.

CHAPTER TWENTY-FIVE

Collins grabbed me around the waist and wrestled me onto the table again. "Now stay there!"

Will Haines looked on, his expression still neutral.

Tears stung my eyes. I had trusted this man, begun to love him even.

Collins turned to Haines. "How'd you find this place?" A little surprise in his voice, but no fear, as if he were asking how the sheriff had located such a nice restaurant.

"I'm a detective." His voice was hard. "I detected it."

My head was spinning. Was he or wasn't he in league with my captors?

Haines looked my way. Something flitted across his face, so fast I couldn't read it. "I got the dog," he said in a flat voice.

My chest and throat constricted. I couldn't breathe.

"Good," Collins said. He turned back to me. "One last time, who did you tell about what you found out?"

"I didn't tell anyone but him." I jerked my head in Haines' direction. "I trusted that the *sheriff*," venom dripped from the word, "would handle things."

Haines gestured toward me with the barrel of his pistol. "I don't think she blabbed to anybody else. I told her to keep what she found out to herself, except to tell me."

My throat closed and tears welled. He *had* said words to that effect. For my own protection, I'd assumed at the time.

Collins grunted. He stared at me for a moment. "Okay. We

can get rid of her now."

I felt lightheaded.

Frank Larson was suddenly standing at the end of table, glaring down at me. Blood dribbled from his smashed nose. He unbuckled his belt and whipped it off. "I'm gettin' some payback outta her first."

Bile rose in my throat.

Cold metal pressed against my temple, a gun barrel. The sheriff's face hovered over mine. "I got first dibs. It's the least you all can do after I had to pretend to like her."

The room went fuzzy, a prism of colors creating an aura around the edges.

Crapola! I'm fainting.

CHAPTER TWENTY-SIX

I was only out for a few seconds. Just long enough for Frank Larson to get a good grip on my jeans' legs and yank. I woke up to the sensation of the button giving. It flew across the room.

Inanely, my first thought was, *I should have zipped my jeans.* But there'd been no time for such niceties when I'd believed there was a gator, or worse, in my kitchen.

"Back off, Larson." The words a growl next to my ear. The cold ring of steel was no longer pressed against my temple. Haines' pistol was now pointed at Frank Larson's heart.

Confusion, relief and anger did a strange dance in my chest. Was he a good guy after all, undercover maybe? Then why'd he let things get so far?

Collins stepped forward, waggling Frank's gun back and forth. "Nobody's doing anything that leaves marks or evidence. It's gotta looked like she banged her head when her car ran into that tree, and then wandered into the Forest and got lost."

Haines took a step away from the table. He glanced briefly at me, his face unreadable. His gun barrel was now pointed toward the floor.

Frank also backed up a little. He cackled. "Maybe some critter'll come along and chew on her some before she's found."

I gagged and turned my head away from all of them.

Beams of light blasted across the dim room. Footsteps pounded. Voices shouted, "Halt! Don't move!"

I jerked my head back around. Collins was now down on one

knee, a hand clasping the other wrist, the gun gone from his hand.

Haines stood over him.

It took a beat for my brain to process what was happening. The cavalry had arrived. At least, I hoped it was the cavalry. I seemed to be a poor judge lately of who wore the white hats.

A weight suddenly dropped over my entire body. I could see nothing but a blur of blue chambray. "I'm so sorry," Will's voice murmured in my ear. Then he shouted, "I've got the victim."

Warmth swelled in my chest and I almost burst into tears. He was shielding me with his body. Then my gut twisted. Where was Larson? Did he have another gun?

My body bucked of its own accord, wanting to flip over and shield Will.

Scuffling noises and grunting for a few seconds. Then a male voice began reciting the Miranda warning I'd heard often enough on cop shows.

Pent-up breath whooshed out of me.

Will pushed his torso up off of me with one hand and started unbuttoning his shirt.

What the…?

He slid off the side of the table facing the door. It hit me that he was blocking others from seeing my bare legs. I felt the flutter of cloth against my skin. He'd covered me with his shirt.

I burst into tears. He was definitely one of the good guys.

"Any female officers present?" he called out as he untied my hands. He took one of them and squeezed it.

I cleared my throat to dislodge the lump that had suddenly appeared there. "Not necessary. You're doing fine."

CHAPTER TWENTY-SEVEN

Will found me amongst the jumble of parked vehicles and people tromping around on the dirt road. I was sitting on the EMT's gurney, a blanket over my bare legs. The EMT clucked to herself as she extracted bits of automotive glass from my face and neck.

I winced. "Am I going to need stitches?" I asked, just as Will appeared next to her.

"Don't think so," the EMT said. "I'll put some butterfly bandages on a couple of the cuts."

"Good," I said. "Then I won't need to go to the hospital."

The EMT grimaced. "I should try to talk you into it, but realistically, no, you don't need to go."

Will picked up his shirt from where it lay beside me on the gurney. He draped it over one shoulder, drawing my eyes to his well-defined pecs.

Despite the circumstances, my nether regions sat up and took notice. Heat crept up my cheeks. I ducked my head.

When I glanced up, the corners of his mouth were twitching as he fought a grin.

Relief washed through me. He wasn't mad, or at least not totally furious. He hadn't said much when he'd carried me out of the shack. Just delivered me to the EMTs and handed me his phone. "Better call your neighbor. She's frantic."

"Edna Mayfair?"

"No, the black lady next door."

"Oh, baby," Mrs. Wells had gushed into the phone–I'd never

thought of her as a gusher before. "I'm so glad he found you. You're not hurt, are you? Is Buddy okay? I tried to call you but it went to your voicemail. I didn't know what to think when I saw that man taking Buddy away."

Crapola! The missed call when I'd left my phone in the car at the grocery store. And I'd ignored the poor woman's attempts to stop me and warn me at the house.

Fools rush in… My mother's voice, singing off-key in my head.

I'd thanked Sherie Wells for her concern and then proceeded to fib to her. I'd said we were both fine, even though I didn't know for sure at that point how, or even where, Buddy was.

Still didn't. My chest and throat tightened. I looked up at Will. "Buddy? He's lost out there in the woods somewhere."

Will smiled and he pulled his right hand forward. In it was a piece of old twine. Attached to the other end was a rather bedraggled black dog.

"Buddy!"

He woofed softly and I started crying. He jumped up, planting muddy front paws in my lap, and licked my face. My tears turned to laughter.

"Hey, I just cleaned there," the EMT protested.

"Sorry. Down, boy," I said, although I could have used a few more doggy kisses.

The EMT went at the cuts again, the antiseptic stinging like crazy. But I was so relieved I didn't care.

"So you were one of the good guys after all," I said to Will.

"Yeah. I was trying to stall them until the others arrived." He handed over the end of the twine and slipped his shirt on. But he didn't button it.

I surreptitiously enjoyed the view. It was a great distraction from the EMT's ministrations.

"When I got to your house," Will said, "I knew you couldn't have heard my message. I got here as fast as I could."

"Message?"

"Yeah. Uh…" He glanced sideways at the EMT.

I got it. He didn't want to say too much in front of her.

"All done," she said. "Can I have my gurney back then, if you're not going to the hospital?"

Will helped me down and steadied me as we made our way awkwardly to his cruiser, me hanging onto my improvised and now muddy blanket skirt with one hand. Buddy walked beside me, as close as he could get without tripping me up.

Will sat me down in the passenger seat of his car. Buddy wiggled up against my knee and put his head in my lap. I stroked his soft ears.

Will stood, leaning on the open door while we talked. "Collins approached me soon after I became sheriff, with a thinly veiled offer of bribes if I became his lackey. I politely turned him down. But after Jimmy died, I decided to use that to get on the inside. I told Collins I'd figured out who had killed his sister, and for a modest monthly supplement to my salary, I'd keep it to myself. The bribe money's been going into an escrow account, and Agent Marlow of the Florida Department of Law Enforcement has known what I was doing all along."

My chest constricted. "Wasn't that risky? What if Collins had decided to kill you?"

He shrugged, making the unbuttoned shirt part and inadvertently showing off his tight abdomen–not exactly a six pack but no fat to speak of either. I felt a little dizzy.

"I figured he'd prefer to have me in his pocket," Will said, "rather than risk whoever might get elected to take my place. Not to mention the high probability that he'd get caught if he killed me. Law enforcement tends to work a little harder when it's one of their own who's been murdered."

I nodded. Buddy whimpered softly. I scratched under his chin.

"Collins called me this morning, wanted to meet. He told me he was going to need my help this afternoon, but he wouldn't say for what. I wondered why he'd dragged me all the way up to Belleview to tell me something he could've said over the phone."

So I hadn't imagined Will's voice in that crowded grocery store.

"Then he called me about a half hour later and told me to head up toward Ocala. He'd call again with more directions. That's when I got it. He'd wanted me up in Belleview to make sure I was out of the way, because they were going to do what Collins had been threatening for a while. To, quote, 'take care of that meddlin' Banks woman.'" He made air quotes, causing the shirt to part again.

I realized my mouth was hanging open. I quickly closed it.

"I'd told him I was getting cozy with you to find out what you knew. I think all this," Will gestured to encompass the shack and road, "was partly to test my loyalty. Would I stand by and let you be killed?"

"Why didn't you arrest him before this?" I was a little irked. If he'd done so, neither Buddy nor I would have gone through all this trauma.

"Because he's never actually said out loud that he'd killed his sister. And I didn't have a clear motive. Still don't." He grimaced. "I was praying I'd get to you before they did. I called, but I got your voicemail. My heart about stopped when I got to your house and found the door unlocked and nobody home."

He must have called while I was in the shower. What crappy timing!

"Your neighbor saved the day. She said some man carried Buddy out of your house, and the dog looked to be real sick or maybe dead. I recognized her description of the man as Dwayne Snyder, so I alerted Agent Marlow. He put out a statewide BOLO on Snyder and his truck–"

"What's a BOLO?"

"Be on the lookout for. Snyder's truck was spotted, and a Marion County detective in an unmarked car tailed it. Good thing too. If we'd waited for Collins to give me my final instructions…" His voice trailed off.

The cavalry might not have gotten here in time.

"But the detective had to keep his distance until he had some back-up. I caught up with him at a fork in the road not far from here. He didn't know which way they'd gone. We were about to split up and search, when Buddy came barreling out of the woods. He saw me, barked, then turned around and took off. Led us right to the shack. But then I had to stall until the back-up got here."

I leaned over and hugged Buddy's neck. "My hero."

Will cleared his throat.

I looked up at him. "I mean, you're both my heroes."

But he was shaking his head slightly. "What the heck were you thinking?"

I dropped my gaze. "I didn't think, just took off. They'd left a note. Told me to come to some bogus address or they'd kill Buddy."

I grimaced and looked up at Will. "When I realized I'd forgotten my phone, sanity returned. But they were waiting for me at an abandoned building. How'd they know I'd stop there?"

"They didn't. They were probably following you, waiting for an opportunity to get you out of your car."

I felt a spasm of grief for my poor little car. "But why didn't Snyder just wait for me to come home and take us both?"

Will shrugged. "That was probably the original plan, to nab you both. But you weren't there and they had no idea when you'd get back. I doubt Snyder thought of leaving the note. Collins probably dictated it to him over the phone. Figured he'd get you out of Mayfair, away from any nosy neighbors."

Thank God for nosy neighbors!

Will patted Buddy's head. "I really hated having to pretend that I'd shot him, but I needed you to believe I was in with them. Otherwise, you might have done something to tip them off."

I understood the logic of what he was saying, but my eyes stung at the memory of those awful feelings of betrayal.

Will was shaking his head again. "I get how much you care about your animals, Marcia. I'm a dog person myself. But when we found your car at that building and it was all bashed up–" His voice caught. He stopped and swallowed hard, his Adam's apple bobbing in his tanned throat. "I thought you were badly hurt, maybe even dead."

My chest ached. I reached out a hand, touched his shirt.

He took my hand and lifted it to his mouth. His warm lips on my fingertips sent a zing down my arm and through my body.

"Please don't do that to me again," he said in a soft voice.

I was trying to think of something to say, distracted by the afterglow of the zing and the random glimpses of chest and abdomen.

He let go of my hand and started buttoning his shirt. "I'd better get back to work."

A groan escaped my throat.

He leaned down. "You can admire my naked chest any time you like," he whispered, his breath warm against my ear. "But I'd prefer it to be in the privacy of one of our homes."

Heat shot up through my body, all the way to the top of my head.

He pulled back a little and put a finger under my chin to raise my face up. His eyes looked worried. "You, uh, are still interested, aren't you?"

My cheeks were burning, but I grinned at him. "Yes, sir. I am."

"Good. I'll get somebody to take you and Buddy home." He leaned in again. This time he brushed his lips against mine. "To be continued." He turned and walked away.

EPILOGUE

One sunny day in late March, I left early for Collinsville. Will and I had a lunch date, but I had something I needed to do first. I'd been putting off this assignment from my counselor for way too long.

In the parking lot of the Collinsville Baptist Church, I stepped out of my car, then reached back in to retrieve the wild flowers I'd gathered from the roadside in front of my house.

Buddy whined softly in the backseat. "Don't worry, boy. I'm not leaving you."

I once again thanked God and the universe for Mattie. She'd talked the board of trustees into letting me buy Buddy, and had even set up a payment plan that only stretched my budget slightly more than usual.

I opened the back door and unsnapped Buddy from his safety harness so he could jump out.

The Florida spider grass was already making significant inroads across the raw dirt of the graves. I might not have found them, if it hadn't been for the woman standing beside them, a small child in her arms.

Sheila Collins greeted me in a soft voice. She put Ida Mae down on her feet, and the toddler patted Buddy on the head, a little too vigorously.

The dog must have remembered her because he tolerated her affectionate abuse.

"I'm sorry," Sheila said.

I shook my head. “Not your doing.”

“I can’t say our marriage was a happy one, but I never dreamed he could kill his own sister.”

I was quiet. What could I say, that greed was a powerful motive. Greed and the desire to stay out of jail. It had all come out at her husband’s arraignment. Turned out his motives had nothing to do with his affair with Carol Reynolds.

Collins had been embezzling money from the bank for years, ever since he’d taken it over from his grandfather. Julie had caught on and was collecting evidence before blowing the whistle.

So brother John had paid his buddy Frank to kill her, while making sure he had an airtight alibi. Oh, he’d failed to mention the payoff at the hearing, making it sound like Frank had acted on his own.

But Frank Larson had already accepted a plea bargain. To avoid the death penalty, he’d spilled his guts, as had Dwayne Snyder, who’d been charged as an accessory to both Julie’s murder and my kidnapping.

Frank had found Jimmy out cold on the floor and figured it was the perfect set up to frame him. It was one of the few times Larson had a fairly bright idea. He’d pretended to Julie that he was there to help, then followed her into the bedroom, closed the door and attacked her. Julie had fought him but he’d gotten a hand over her mouth early on, keeping her from screaming.

Buddy hadn’t reacted to all that because he wouldn’t have understood why Julie had suddenly gone quiet in the next room. But when Frank went out to his truck, came back with a beer and poured it on Jimmy, the dog went ballistic.

Frank’s sleeve had caught on Buddy’s collar as he’d fought the dog off, then he’d bolted out of the house leaving the front door ajar.

Will had told me privately that Frank had also admitted to taunting Jimmy about Julie’s affair, while he was a captive audience in that jail cell. That had most likely been the final straw that tipped Jimmy over the edge.

And now this little girl in front of me was an orphan.

"What are you going to do from here?" I asked Sheila.

"I'll raise Ida Mae, and I'll try to keep her from ever knowing that her father was accused of killing her mama. Jimmy was a hero. He deserves to have his daughter's memory of him untainted."

Good luck with that in a small town, I thought but didn't say out loud.

Sheila had apparently had the same thought. "I'm moving to Orlando once my daughter's off to college in the fall. My sister lives there." She smiled for the first time. "My daughter wants to take over the bank once she learns the ropes."

"So you think the bank will survive the scandal?"

"Yeah. It's the only one in town. People aren't gonna want to drive to Polk City or Lakeland. And John had invested most of the money he'd stolen, so I was able to make restitution."

I nodded and ruffled Ida Mae's soft curls. At least the child would never have to worry about finances.

She looked up at me with saucer eyes. Then she said, "Buddy," as clear as could be.

I crouched down next to her. She banged on the poor dog's head again. He licked her arm.

"Yes, Buddy," I pushed past the lump in my throat.

"Say goodbye to Miss Marcia," Sheila said.

The child threw her arms around me, almost knocking me on my butt. Warmth spread through my chest. I squeezed her gently.

Then she let go and slammed Buddy on the head one last time. "Bye, bye."

Her aunt lifted her into her arms, then picked her way through the graves toward the church parking lot.

My eyes stung as I watched them go. Maybe rug rats weren't so bad after all.

Crapola! Where'd that *thought come from?*

~~~~<>~~~~
~~~~

AUTHOR'S NOTES

If you enjoyed this book, please take a moment to leave a short review on Amazon and/or other online book retailers. Reviews really help with sales, and sales provide funds for more books! You can find the links for the book's page on these retailers at http://misteriopress.com/misterio-press-bookstore/#kassandra-lamb

We at *misterio press* pride ourselves on providing our readers with top-quality reads. All of our books are proofread multiple times by several pairs of eyes, but proofreaders are human. If you found errors in this book, please email the author at lambkassandra3@gmail.com so they can be corrected. Thank you!

First let me pass around some much deserved gratitude and then I'll share some background tidbits with you, and give you a peek at the next book in the series.

Huge thanks to my wonderful daughter-in-law, romance author, G.G. Andrew, whose thorough critique of the story and comments on all things Millennial were so, so helpful. And much gratitude as well to my good friend and partner in crime over at *misterio press*, Shannon Esposito. She also read the manuscript in its early stages and helped shape it into a better story, and she advised me on the differences between a regular mystery and a cozy.

Vinnie Hansen of *misterio* also critiqued this story, and her eagle eye caught a bunch of typos. Thank you, Vinnie. And thank you also to fellow mystery writer, Susan Reiss for doing a final check for continuity and to my wonderful brother for reading and commenting on the guy stuff. And hugs to my husband for doing the final proofread. (He didn't find any more typos, Vinnie!)

As always, my undying gratitude to Marcy Kennedy, my editor *extraordinaire*, who has taught me so much about writing.

And last but not least, an extra special thank you to my friend,

Angi, whose support kept me going in the early stages of my writing career. And for this book, she was even more crucial. She has a PhD after her name and is currently conducting research to scientifically document the multitude of ways that service dogs help veterans suffering from PTSD cope with and overcome their symptoms.

She and I went to lunch one day and I was bouncing up and down in my chair, telling her about this great new idea I'd had for a mystery series all about a dog trainer who's training service dogs for veterans. She got this weird little smile on her face and said, "You'll never believe the research I just started doing?"

The universe is extremely generous at times.

Angi advised me on training signals and protocols and such. Any mistakes are mine. The organization that Marcia works for in the series is fictional, but I am trying to be as true as possible to how the dogs are really trained. I do occasionally have to bend reality a bit to make the stories work, however. A true service dog trainer would have never, ever left Max with Pete Sanchez that early on in the training process. But I needed to get Max out of the way so the house would be empty the day the alligator came visiting.

Gators, by the way, almost never come inside houses in Florida, even in rural areas. But they might mosey into your backyard if you live near a body of water or go for a dip in your pool if it isn't fenced in. And yes, there are folks in Florida who specialize in removing them and other unwelcome critters from your premises.

The cities of Ocala and Lakeland and the towns of Polk City and Belleview are real, but the town of Mayfair is fictional as is Collinsville, Florida, where Sheriff Hunky enforces the law. There are several Collinsvilles around the country, including one in Connecticut where a gruesome true crime spree occurred, but best I could tell from my Google search, there is no Collinsville, Florida. If there is, my apologies to those townspeople for portraying them as rather narrow-minded.

The Ocala National Forest is also quite real, and has indeed been known to swallow unwitting hikers and campers whole.

Book 2 in the series stars Lacy from this book. It's title is *Arsenic and Young Lacy*, and I hope to have it out by the end of the summer (early fall at the latest). Here's a sneak peak:

ARSENIC AND YOUNG LACY, A MARCIA BANKS AND BUDDY MYSTERY

"Mar-ci-a," the frustrated voice coming out of my phone emphasized every syllable of my name. "What the *devil* have you gotten yourself into now?"

The voice was that of my, uh, boyfriend… um, male friend… man friend… lover?

Hmm, tall, hunky Will Haines was definitely not a boy, and male friend sounded way too platonic. Man friend was kind of primitive–brought up some interesting images of us taking turns hauling each other off to some cave.

And sadly, we did not qualify for lover status, although it hadn't been for lack of trying, at least recently.

"What do you mean?" I feigned my most innocent tone, and crossed my fingers to boot. Did Millennials still do that? Ever since Will had pointed out that I was not a typical thirty-something, I'd been second guessing myself all over the place.

The sound of air being blown out in a long-suffering sigh. "Why am I getting a BOLO on some guy for a destruction of property charge and your name's on it as the complainant, with some address up in Ocala? *And* it's flagged that the suspect is potentially dangerous."

Crapola. I hadn't realized a be-on-the-lookout bulletin in Marion County would make it all the way to Sheriff Will's desk in Collinsville, a county away.

"Uh, I was helping out, um, a friend."

Well, Rainey Bryant wasn't a friend exactly, although she thought she was. She was my client, or rather the client of the agency for which I train service dogs. And technically it would probably be considered unethical for me to become friends with her, although she seemed to want that to happen.

Yeah, I know, I'm a mess in the relationship department.

Buddy, my black Lab-Rottie mix, whined softly and tilted his head at me with his patented what's-up look. I'd been about to take him for a walk, had the leash in my hand even, when Will called.

"Just a minute, boy."

"You talking to me?"

"No, to Buddy."

"Are you *going* to talk to me?"

"Yeah, I'm just trying to figure out what to say."

"How about the truth."

Ouch!

"Hey, that's not fair. When have I ever lied to you?"

Another sigh. "Your sins tend to be more ones of omission."

Okay, I had to give him that. "Look, it's a long story."

"I've got nothing better to do right now."

I held my hand out, palm parallel to the floor and motioned down. Buddy tilted his head the other way, then complied. I flopped down on my sofa.

"Okay, but this has to do with a client so some of it's confidential. You have to keep it to yourself." I paused for breath before plunging in.

I really liked Rainey Bryant, from the first time I met her. Although later, I would wonder why. She was bright and friendly, and despite all that she'd been through, there was an innocent, child-like quality about her.

And she'd been through plenty. For one thing, she was an Army nurse so she'd survived basic training, although perhaps hers wasn't as rigorous physically as that of a woman who'd volunteered for the infantry.

I didn't know, since I wasn't totally up on how such things worked inside the military. I was pretty familiar , however, with how things worked, or didn't, after people got out of the military.

The service dogs I train for veterans who suffer from PTSD should be like a prosthesis or a wheelchair for physical injuries, paid for by the Veterans Administration. But they aren't always. Fortunately, the agency I train for has grant money for scholarships, so those vets who can't afford the ten-thousand dollar fee can still get the service dog they need.

Rainey didn't know that I knew that she was the recipient of one of those scholarships. Mattie Jones, the woman I work for, had accidentally let it slip.

I'd met Rainey in person for the first time when I took her potential service dog to her house to introduce them to each other. It was something Mattie insisted on–make sure the animal and recipient are compatible before starting the expensive training process.

At that point, I was officially Lacy's foster mom. Mattie had arrangements with several local rescue shelters that allowed her trainers to take dogs on a trial basis.

Lacy, a mostly white collie-Alaskan husky mix, was a little yappy, but otherwise she had the right temperament for a service animal–intelligent, people-oriented, eager to please.

Rainey loved her at first sight....

Stay tuned! I'm writing as fast as I can.

ABOUT THE AUTHOR

Kassandra Lamb has never been able to decide which she loves more, psychology or writing. In college, she realized that writers need a day job in order to eat, so she studied psychology. After a career as a psychotherapist and college professor, she is now retired and can pursue her passion for writing. She spends most of her time in an alternate universe with her characters. The portal to this universe, aka her computer, is located in Florida, where her husband and dog catch occasional glimpses of her. She and her husband spend part of each summer in her native Maryland, where her Kate Huntington series is based.

Kass is currently working on Book 2 in the Marcia Banks and Buddy Mysteries. She has eight books out in the Kate Huntington Mystery series, plus three Kate on Vacation novellas (somewhat lighter reads along the lines of cozy mysteries). The next Kate on Vacation novella, *Missing on Maui*, should be out this summer.

To read and see more about Kassandra and her characters you can go to http://kassandralamb.com. Be sure to sign up for the newsletter there to get a heads up about new releases, plus special offers and bonuses for subscribers. (New subscribers get a free e-copy of the first Kate on Vacation novella.)

Kass's e-mail is lambkassandra3@gmail.com and she loves hearing from readers! She's also on Facebook (http://www.facebook.com/kassandralambauthor) and hangs out some on Twitter @KassandraLamb. She blogs about psychological topics and other random things at http://misteriopress.com.

Please check out these other great *misterio press* series:

Mulitple Motives (Kate Huntington Mysteries)
by Kassandra Lamb

Karma's A Bitch (Pet Psychic Mysteries)
by Shannon Esposito

Maui Widow Waltz (Islands of Aloha Mysteries)
by JoAnn Bassett

The Metaphysical Detective (Riga Hayworth Mysteries)
by Kirsten Weiss

Dangerous and Unseemly (Concordia Wells Mysteries)
by K.B. Owen

Murder, Honey (Carol Sabala Mysteries)
by Vinnie Hansen

Steam and Sensibility
(Sensibility Grey Steampunk Mysteries)
by Kirsten Weiss

Made in the USA
Middletown, DE
03 December 2019

79937967R00136